PUFFIN CANADA

HANNAH WATERS AND
THE DAUGHTER OF
JOHANN SEBASTIAN BACH

BARBARA NICKEL's young adult novel *The Secret Wish of Nannerl Mozart* was shortlisted for the Mr. Christie's Book Award, the Geoffrey Bilson Award for Historical Fiction for Young People, and the Red Cedar Young Readers' Choice Award. It has also been optioned for film by Ellen Freyer Productions in Los Angeles. As well as being a children's writer, Nickel is an award-winning and widely anthologized poet for adults and has had fiction and non-fiction pieces published in many literary journals and magazines. She lives in Yarrow, British Columbia, with her husband and two children.

Also by Barbara Nickel

The Secret Wish of Nannerl Mozart

From the Top of a Grain Elevator
(poetry)

The Gladys Elegies
(poetry)

Concerto for Two Violins by J.S. Bach, excerpt from autograph copy

Hannah Waters

and the daughter of

Johann Sebastian Bach

barbara nickel

PUFFIN
CANADA

PUFFIN CANADA

Published by the Penguin Group

Penguin Group (Canada), 90 Eglinton Avenue East, Suite 700, Toronto, Ontario, Canada M4P 2Y3
(a division of Pearson Canada Inc.)

Penguin Group (USA) Inc., 375 Hudson Street, New York, New York 10014, U.S.A.
Penguin Books Ltd, 80 Strand, London WC2R 0RL, England
Penguin Ireland, 25 St Stephen's Green, Dublin 2, Ireland (a division of Penguin Books Ltd)
Penguin Group (Australia), 250 Camberwell Road, Camberwell, Victoria 3124, Australia
(a division of Pearson Australia Group Pty Ltd)
Penguin Books India Pvt Ltd, 11 Community Centre, Panchsheel Park, New Delhi – 110 017, India
Penguin Group (NZ), cnr Airborne and Rosedale Roads, Albany, Auckland 1310, New Zealand
(a division of Pearson New Zealand Ltd)
Penguin Books (South Africa) (Pty) Ltd, 24 Sturdee Avenue, Rosebank, Johannesburg 2196,
South Africa

Penguin Books Ltd, Registered Offices: 80 Strand, London WC2R 0RL, England

First published in Penguin Canada paperback by Penguin Group (Canada),
a division of Pearson Canada Inc., 2005
Published in this edition, 2006

1 2 3 4 5 6 7 8 9 10   (OPM)

Copyright © Barbara Nickel, 2005

Excerpts from *Alligator Pie* (Macmillan of Canada, 1974, Key Porter Books, 2001).
Copyright © 1974 Dennis Lee. With permission of the author.

Copperplate engraving from Martin Zeiller's *Topographia Germaniae, Volume on
Upper Saxony*, Frankfurt am Main, 1650. Courtesy of Bach-Gedenkstätte, Köthen.

Concerto for Two Violins by J.S. Bach reproduced with permission
from Biblioteka Jagiellońska, Kraków, Poland.

Manufactured in the U.S.A.

ISBN-10: 0-14-305079-6
ISBN-13: 978-0-14-305079-7

Library and Archives Canada Cataloguing in Publication data available upon request

Visit the Penguin Group (Canada) website at **www.penguin.ca**

Special and corporate bulk purchase rates available; please see
www.penguin.ca/corporatesales or call 1-800-399-6858, ext. 477 or 474

For you, Mom

Hannah Waters

❧ and the daughter of ❧

Johann Sebastian Bach

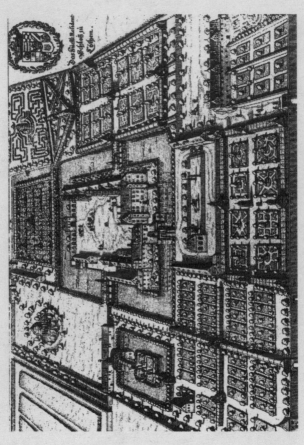

A bird's eye view of Prince Leopold's castle, with the maze in the upper right corner.

One

Catharina

I LISTEN TO MAMA sing as we beat Papa's shirts in the river. Her voice runs like silk in the sun over the water and slides with shadows into the reeds. It's Lise's day off, and the well in Cöthen is dry, so Mama and I must do the washing here. I give Papa's sleeve a twist and look at Mama bent over, braids coiled up on her head and shining like a crown. She sees me, smiles, nods for me to join in. Finding a harmony to Mama's melody is as easy as kneading dough. It really is her song. Papa composed it. One night he lit three candles and said, "Tonight, a piece for my wife!" and the next morning I peeked into the kitchen and saw him give the sheet of music to her. Then they kissed for quite a space and I was afraid they'd see me so I ducked away. The sheet says "For Maria Barbara" at the top. Even Mama's name is like music.

She stops singing and turns away. "Come," she calls, climbing the muddy bank with her heap of clothes. "These must be dried and ironed today. Papa's concert tomorrow—"

"Can't we stay here and rest a little?" I ask, plodding in the mud after her. It's hard to keep up. If we were birds, Mama would be a lark, so small, with that huge voice trilling out through the leaves. I'd be the duck on the bank, always clumsy in my chores.

"These shirts, your poor papa, the boys—"

"Always the boys. Tante Lena's with them." I have the great honour to be an older sister to a parcel of rascals aged nine, five, and four—Wilhelm, Carl, and little chubby Johann. "Please, Mama? I'm sure they're all sitting around the table, not saying a word and twiddling their fat thumbs."

"Catharina Dorthea," Mama begins to scold, then bursts into laughter. "More like hanging from the trees shrieking, or wearing my poor sister's nerves to the bone." She hesitates for a moment. "Oh, all right," she says, sinking into the grass. "But only for a few minutes, mind."

She means only a few minutes—I can tell from her voice. I'm just glad to be alone with Mama. She takes a sheet of Papa's music from her satchel, and the wooden board that sits on her lap. She always carries music with her wherever she goes, in case there's a spare minute to copy his rough scribbles onto a fresh sheet of paper, a good copy that the court musicians can use. Of course, the prince pays Herr Colm, the copyist, a good many thalers to do this, but there's never enough time because Papa composes heaps more music than there are hands to copy. Mama takes a quill pen from her velvet drawstring bag and pulls the cork from a pot of ink.

I look over her shoulder at the neat black lines and circles and draw a deep breath. She is copying ... *the* piece. In my head, I can hear the two solo violins criss-crossing and looping around each other like paths in a forest. My right hand is shaking. I grasp it with the other and try to make it stop. Stupid hand, to think you can move with Mama's grace on a page. You'd dribble ink all over Papa's glorious music! "What is it this time?" I ask, all innocence. She thinks I know nothing.

"Oh, the score for the Concerto for Two Violins. See, here are the two solos."

I remember when Papa first tried this. I was supposed to be asleep, but even above Wilhelm's snores, I could hear the notes from Papa's violin

3

drifting down through the ceiling like snowflakes. I've stayed awake through many nights listening to Papa try his compositions, but I'll never forget that night. I pulled my quilt closer and looked out the window at the stars and the half moon, and this empty space inside me started filling up with music that I wanted to sing. I soaked up each note—the lines were in my head because Papa played them over and over again through the night. When the rooster crowed and we had to get up, I slapped my feet down and I didn't mind the icy floor because the music was telling me, *Stand up! Stretch! Walk through that door without a stumble! Sing out in morning prayers!*

And as we gathered around the clavichord I held my head up and for the first time looked Papa straight in the eye and then kept my head up for a whole song. After breakfast, when I was clearing away the dishes, I heard him say to Mama as he was walking out the door to the palace, "Our girl sings not badly! Perhaps she's a true Bach after all!"

Not that I've been able to keep my eyes off the floor in morning prayers since. Yesterday I was back to watching our cat, Lumpi, twist herself around the clavichord's legs. But who knows what else could happen if I learn this piece well enough, keep it singing through my head every day? Now Mama's hands make the little circles and lines, and I make a game of singing the notes in my head before they appear on the page, the sun warming my back.

"The boys will have toppled the house by now." Mama puts the tail on an eighth note with a flourish and begins to put her things away.

I want to coax a few more minutes, but I pick up the laundry basket instead. There is a little mud on one of Papa's silky cuffs. I must have dragged it on the way up the bank. I check to see that Mama isn't looking and furiously start rubbing. It won't go away.

"Oh, Catharina." She is behind me, her voice gentle. She takes the shirt and the soap for washing. I follow her back down the bank.

⌦

I sweep and sweep the rehearsal chamber. Soon Papa's musicians, the Cöthen Court Capelle of Prince Leopold, will come with their violins and cellos and flutes and bassoons and oboes, sit down in the chairs I have polished, and begin to play. I mustn't leave a speck of dust, not even one of Lumpi's black or white hairs, for then Herr Spiess will sneeze and interrupt the music and Papa will be angry. Herr Spiess plays the violin and sneezes at all cats and dust and is the most important man, next to Papa, of course. Papa leads them all, sitting at the harpsichord or playing the viola or the violin.

My hand is shaking as I set down the broom and pick up my candle to light the others fixed in their holders around the walls. Soon Papa's men will be here! I have to stand on tiptoe to reach. I mustn't spill the wax. I mustn't soot the walls. I light the last candle just as the clop of horses and carriages comes up the street. I peer down and see Herr Spiess knock on the door.

I turn around quickly and inspect the room before making my escape. The candlelight flicks shadows over the polished wooden chairs and stands. All is perfect—not a speck of dust to be found—and Lumpi has gone into hiding. I close my eyes for just a minute and imagine the music that will echo through this room, dance with the shadows in the flickering of light.

A sneeze. Herr Spiess! But how can he be up here already, and why is he sneezing? I run to grab my broom.

"Is this your eldest, Johann?" Herr Spiess walks into the room and opens his case, takes out his violin. "She's grown so big since I last saw her." He turns to me. "How old would you be now, girl?"

Papa nods toward me. I hold my broom and tremble at the door, run my eye along the parquet, each wooden strip. "Tell Herr Spiess your age."

"I … I …" Something has caught hold of my tongue and won't let go. It's always been like this with Papa, ever since I can remember. He looms above me with some simple question or command and I turn into a shivering ninny. "Mama!" I call inside my head, hoping she'll somehow sense me through the floorboards and come running up to the rescue.

Some of the other men laugh and talk as they walk with their instruments toward me through the hall. I must leave. I can't leave. "I—"

"She was twelve in December," Papa says to Herr Spiess, "and, it would appear, has precious few words to show for her age." He shakes his head as if he can't believe he's been blessed with such a dunce for a daughter, then turns and shoos me from the room with his glare. "Well, go on, then," his half whisper sends me fleeing down the stairs, through the kitchen where Wilhelm sits at his lessons and Mama and Tante Lena sew. They glance up as I fly past them. I dive into my bed and wrap the quilt around me, grab Lumpi, and hold her close. Later, Mama will come to me and rub my back and make it all better. She knows I need to be alone for a while. In the dark room, I stare up at the stars as above me they tune their instruments and begin to play Papa's music that is like those whirling rows and patterns up there. What if I could sing right in their midst, my voice rising above the violins? Herr Spiess would not believe his ears, nor would Papa, Wilhelm, or Tante Lena. Everyone but Mama would stare at each other in wonder and say, "This voice belongs to Catharina, the dim-witted daughter of the great Johann Sebastian Bach?"

"Is there someone out there," I whisper to Lumpi, "who isn't too scared to speak to her own papa?" Lumpi eyes me in the dark as if she thinks I'm a dim-wit, too. "I don't mean silly boys like Wilhelm or Carl. Someone my age, a girl who can hear me, who understands ..." She purrs as if she knows, and the stars wink and blink as if they, too, have an answer. I wrap my quilt up tight, and the music pulls me into that space just before sleeping where I see a girl, small in stature, but with a very large nose. We're singing Papa's music together.

Take it back to the top. That's what Mom would say. *Back to the top, all through for memory in your mind.* So I ignore the sound of the engine and Peppermint Woman digging through her purse and the woman talking on her cellphone and the kids fooling around in the back. I start all over again at the beginning of the Concerto for Two Violins in D Minor by Johann Sebastian Bach, the Bach Double for short, for about the tenth time since leaving the city. I press my nose against the cold window. Barbed-wire fences race along the blue fields. The hooks are sort of like sixteenth notes, dark and ready to snag just as soon as I look away.

"Don't worry about getting lost in the sixteenths. Just think about the shape of each phrase," Mr. Dekker said at my lesson just a few hours ago, crossing one leg over the other and running his fingers over the strings of his violin. "It'll be a few weeks before we can put it together with the first violin part." He said that a few weeks ago, too, and a few weeks before that. I think he must be getting tired of the likes of me, but he never shows it.

Mr. Dekker is no ordinary teacher. How often does a teacher have a tiny print of *Starry Night*, by

Vincent van Gogh, framed, above the cat dish? I love to watch Penny, his very old, black-and-white, diabetic cat, admire it as she sneezily dines on Kitty Nibbles. I love Mr. Dekker's waiting room, too—it's filled with books about things like gnomes and chocolate and musicians to read while I wait for Bridget the Perfect to finish her lesson.

Take it back to the top, to the solo in the middle of the first page. Come on, chug along, just like this bus. Chug, chug, just one more measure, then up the scale, shift, around the corner and—

"Clear Lake, next stop!"

Around the corner and, and … something on the A string? B flat? C?

Lost again. I'll never get it memorized. I jam my toque down over my ears and grab my backpack stuffed full of music and homework. I'm reaching for my violin from the overhead bin just as the driver turns into town, toppling me into the seat beside Peppermint Woman.

"I'm sorry," I say in my most polite speaking-to-adults voice. She smells like the peppermints she's been unwrapping and some kind of perfume that's a mix of roses and toilet cleaner. Her answer is a sniff and a glare, and I really should just stand up and keep going, but there's stuff I'd like to ask her, so I take a deep breath and dive right in. "What takes you to the city every Monday? We're always on the same bus."

She's slowly unwrapping another peppermint, the swirly-red-and-white kind. "In my day ..." She pops it into her mouth. "In my day, children were ... well, never mind." She snaps her purse shut and begins to pull on her gloves.

"Sorry," I say again, standing up and stepping into the aisle. In her day, children were seen and not heard. I've heard that before—in a book somewhere? Anyway, it's a good thing I didn't live in her day— with my big mouth I'd never have survived. I wonder if she ever gets tired of all those peppermints?

We've pulled up to the bowling alley with the Greyhound sign out in front. I march down the aisle, careful to hold my violin lengthwise in front of me so the strap can't get caught on the seats.

"That's quite a load you've got there," Ms. Dumont says, grinning as she helps me step down to the icy white road. "You be careful, Hannah. It's a real cold one tonight."

"Thanks." Ms. Dumont almost always drives the bus out from the city on my lesson days. She's tall and strong and has the bluest eyes I've ever seen. Once I got a seat near the front and she told me about her family—uncles and cousins and ten brothers and sisters and an old, old grandfather who live out on a big farm near a place called Batoche.

I wrap my scarf around and around until only my eyes show. Then I give my violin case handle a squeeze and set off for home. Last year in Toronto, I'd have been knocked flat walking home down the middle of the road. I can just see myself stepping off the sidewalk on my route from the conservatory to St. George Station, standing with my violin case in the middle of rush hour. Here, there's only the *mwuck, mwuck* sound of my boots on the road, a car here and there, the bark of a dog.

I retie my scarf and breathe into it. It's a trick I've figured out to keep my nose and cheeks from freezing. The thing is, it always works for a while, but then my scarf gets all wet and stiff and just makes things colder. I stop at the old brick post office with the musty smell, where the old men gather to read the obituary notices and talk about how this is the coldest February in ten years. The room with the mailboxes is lit up and warm and never locked. I reach into my pocket for the key, but before I open it I peer into our little silver mailbox. I like to imagine that on the other side instead of the place where workers sort through mail, there's another time, and one day instead of a flyer from Clear Lake Meats with the latest specials on ground beef and farmer sausage, there'll be a very old, thin envelope with curvy handwriting addressed just to me.

Of course, there's not even a regular letter for me, not even from Uncle Ted and Aunt Beth. I tuck a few bills for Dad into my knapsack and trudge down the street, past the curling rink and across the park, down a path that cuts through thigh-deep snow. The Bach Double begins in my head again. I hum it into my scarf, keep the beat with each crunch of snow under my boots. *Energy,* Mom would say. *Each note is a star.* I look up. It's so wide up there, just crammed with stars, but in patterns and rows. Sort of like the Bach Double. One star seems to stand out from the rest, almost pulsing, as if it can hear me, Hannah Waters now of Clear Lake, Saskatchewan, humming myself across the park. It helps me to stamp each boot a little harder on the path, stay in the music without one wrong turn all the way to the door.

"Hey, Dad, I'm home!" I burst inside on the last note of the first section. I'm tempted to give the door a victory slam but remember just in time that it's almost off its hinges. The Door is one of Dad's many projects.

"Dad?" I shove off my boots and trail mitts, scarf, and toque up the stairs that creak with every step. I follow the sound of opera and sanding all the way to the den. "Dad?" I have to raise my voice above the trilling soprano and the electric sander that Dad zooms back and forth over the slivery floorboards. Propped up on an old table beside the radio is Dad's latest purchase in a series: *Do It Yourself Floors.*

I almost trip over a pile of carpet strips on my way to turn down the radio. I hate to admit it, but this room looks even worse than when we moved in last August. Back in September, Dad ripped out all the drywall, meaning to replace the insulation, but then he ran into trouble with the wiring, and other projects just seemed to spring out of nowhere, like the Door and the Floor and the Toilet. Except now this insulation sags around everywhere and winter air seeps between the bare boards. I put my jacket back on. The woman's really going crazy now, almost bursting at the top of her lungs. I hate opera almost as much as organ, but Dad says both are the perfect accompaniment to house renovations.

"Dad, I'm home!" I turn down the volume.

Dad looks up, his face completely blank for a moment, then crinkling into a smile as he shuts off the sander. Mom called this the Shift. "It's Gerhard, shifting in from the Planet of Italian Art to Planet Me," she'd say, laughing and giving him a big kiss. Mom once told me that Dad gets so caught up in what he's doing that it takes a lot to shake his concentration. I wish some of his concentration had been passed along to me. Then maybe I could get through the Bach Double without feeling as if I'm falling off a roller coaster.

Dad picks a few slivers from his beard. "Hannah! And how was Professor Dekker today?"

"Dad! Mr. Dekker, not Professor. Fine."

"And Penny?"

"Fine."

"Bridget the Perfect?"

"Perfect. I heard her ace the Bach Double today, the first violin part at the end of Book 5 and I … Mr. Dekker says I …"

I wish I hadn't said anything about the Bach Double. Dad pushes up his glasses and leads the way around piles of old drywall. He thinks I didn't see his face go blank and shift to Planet Mom, but I caught it, all right.

"And what did the good professor with the aging art critic for a cat have to say about the Bach Double?"

"He said it'll be another few weeks before I can …
can …"

Somehow I just can't finish that same sentence
for the third week in a row. I follow Dad into the
kitchen. He's clanging around with the pots, filling
up one with water for the spaghetti.

"Next week," I carry on, before he's done and
silence can fill up the big, bare kitchen. "I'll practise
extra, extra hard this week and next week he'll say
I'm ready. I just know it."

"Of course, of course." Dad peels an onion.
"There's no rush. Rome wasn't built in a day, you
know." He's crying from the onion. He always does,
even with his thick glasses as shields. I hand him
the dishtowel.

I wonder if he's remembering the way the slow
movement of the Bach Double sounded three years
ago at Mom's funeral when Mom's friends from the
orchestra played it. I bet he's remembering the rain
that day, how it wouldn't stop, and how it sounded
against the stained-glass windows of the cathedral,
drifting in and out of Mom's favourite piece in the
world.

"What'll it be tonight?" I run over to the bookshelf, the first piece of furniture we moved into
this old house and filled up with novels, books of

poetry, books about different painters (that's where I first found *Starry Night*, before I saw it above Penny's dish), and, of course, books from Dad's *How To* series. "No critical theory allowed in here!" he shouted as we unloaded the boxes. All his books with the long, boring titles went down to the basement.

Last June, after Dad retired early from the university where he'd taught literature for as long as I can remember, and as soon as I finished school, we cleared out of the house on Howland Avenue, packed up everything except the grand piano, and got ready to move into this old house that Dad inherited from his family ages ago. Uncle Ted, Dad's brother from Kitchener, drove us all the way to Saskatchewan because Dad can't drive and a long time ago vowed he never would if he could help it.

The music selection blaring over the long, hot stretches past Winnipeg kept switching between country oldies and opera. "Can't we listen to something normal?" I kept asking, but Uncle Ted says a day isn't complete without a little country to ease it up, and Dad says opera is the perfect accompaniment to driving through the prairies.

"A clean break," he sang out the window. "No more classes, no more students, no more papers to grade, just this!" He made a big sweep with his arm toward a field that was the most amazing blue.

"Well, Dad, what'll it be? How about a little …" I run my finger over the spines of the books in the poetry section, stand on tiptoe, and look for something to cheer him up. "A little … *Alligator Pie*!" I grab the book and settle onto my reading stool by the stove.

"Excellent." Dad chops a green pepper.

"'Alligator pie, alligator pie,'" I begin to chant, snapping my fingers and moving with the beat.

"'If I don't get some I think I'm gonna die,'" Dad joins in, chopping along in rhythm.

"'Give away the green grass, give away the sky,'" I say, then jump off my stool and start grooving around the kitchen. "'But don't give away my alligator pie.'" By the time we reach "Alligator Soup," Dad's beating on the spaghetti pot with the spoon, I'm clanging pot-lid cymbals and standing on the stool singing the words at the top of my lungs as if I'm an opera singer.

"'But don't give away my alligator soup.'" We finish together and I leap off the stool and crash to the floor. Then Dad starts the whole thing over with "carburetor" instead of "alligator," and I dance around again, the words just rolling along and mixing with the smells of mushrooms and onions and oregano. When it's over, I settle back on my stool and start in on "Wiggle to the Laundromat," then one goofy poem after another, as steam from the boiling spaghetti rises to the tick of the clock, and Dad just stirs on and on, the hint of a smile on his face.

I escape to my room after supper to practise, but my violin won't stay in tune. It must have been all that knocking around on the bus, plus this freezing, dry air. I have to stop and turn a peg to keep the string at a steady pitch, but it won't budge, and when I finally do get it to move, the whole thing slips and makes the string go limp.

"Dumb cold room, stupid dry weather," I say out loud. I jam my violin down into the velvet-lined case. *Gently. Treat your instrument as you would a baby.* I remember Mom wiping a soft flannel cloth over the fingerboard, then around its shoulders to the neck. *Gently.*

"Shut up, Mom," I whisper under my breath, balling up the cloth in my fist and squeezing as hard as I can. My violin's nothing special. Just a three-quarters size, and it's getting too small. I try to erase that picture I have of Mom wiping the violin, but it's been there for so long—ever since I was four and Mom gave me my first real lesson on a sixteenth-size violin the length of a doll. And all through the squawks and fights and me not wanting to practise and trying to get the notes in tune, Mom always held up the Bach Double like a chocolate bar. "When you get to the end of Book 4, you'll get to play this," she said after one lesson when I'd threatened to quit. "The Concerto in D Minor for Two Violins by Johann Sebastian Bach, one of the greatest pieces of music ever written. We'll play it together someday." Then she played some of the notes, and they danced up in the light, glinting with the maple of her old violin.

And then, when I was still on "The Two Grenadiers" in Book 2, Mom went and died and her violin disappeared. Well, not exactly disappeared. I know Dad keeps it somewhere in his room. Under the bed? In a secret closet somewhere? This old house has enough of those. I've often wanted to find it, just open the case and look at it, touch it a little. It's very, very old. Maybe soon I'll be big enough for a full size, and Mom's violin … no, I might as well not even think about it. Even if I just ask to see it, like the last time, something will happen with Dad—I'm not sure what. But I don't think I can stand his silence again.

I loosen my bow and slam my case shut. Who cares if I memorize this stupid piece? I press my nose against the window's cold glass, look out past the bare vines around my window, past the tall pine tree and the curling rink and the grain elevator and out to the darkness and the stars. There's one that keeps pulsing, the one I saw in the park. And I don't really want it to, but the Bach Double in my head begins again.

Two

Hannah

IT'S STILL DARK on the way to school. It snowed last night, and I'm making fresh tracks all the way across the park. I'm not humming the Bach Double anymore, though. All I can think about is if the Town Girls will talk to me today.

In my Grade 6 class, there are the Farm Kids, the Indians, and the Town Kids. On the first day the three main Town Girls came up to me at recess.

"So, in Toronto did you ever go shopping at one of those designer stores? You know, like from *Seventeen*?" asked Melissa. She's the queen. Her braces glinted like jewellery in the sun when she flashed me her "get to know the new girl" smile, staring right at my nose, which is just as big as Dad's and Uncle Ted's.

At my old school in Toronto, I was semi-famous for speeches on endangered species, rights for short people with big noses, eating disorders, global

22

warming, stuff like that. We'd be changing for gym or eating lunch and suddenly—boom!—someone would say something to get me all fired up, and kids would either listen and argue back or laugh and say I was weird. Sometimes I wrote a column called "Hannah's Rant" for the school newspaper. Once I found a copy in the garbage can and someone had changed it to "Hannah the Runt." Lots of kids thought the column and the speeches were a big joke, but at least some people liked it and we had some good talks.

That day in the playground, with Melissa smirking down at my nose, I felt a speech welling up, and even though everything was new and strange I couldn't keep it from bursting out.

"Well, first off, I make a point not to read *Seventeen*," I said, launching right in. "All those skinny models distorting our body image. I'm not about to become anorexic, thank you very much." Melissa had stopped smiling. A thought blipped through my mind that maybe this wasn't exactly going to earn me popularity points, but I was on a roll. "As for designer stores—all the clothes, besides being way overpriced, are meant for girls with figures like stick bugs ..." I finally realized they were staring at me as if I were an alien, so I forced myself to shut

23

up by concentrating on the frayed hem of my jeans. When will I learn to keep my big mouth shut?

"So where did you shop?" giggled Tracy, Melissa's lady-in-waiting. Her dad owns the only department store in town and both drugstores, and I've heard that he owns stores in other towns as well.

I pushed up my glasses. There was no way I was going to tell them that Mom mostly picked up stuff for me at the second-hand place near our house in Toronto and that I've gone on exactly three shopping trips for clothes since she died, with Aunt Beth from Kitchener, who means well but doesn't exactly have designer taste.

Melissa snapped her gum. "So what did you do all the time if you didn't shop? I mean, my mom takes me to the mall in the city almost every weekend."

I wasn't going to tell them about practising violin or going to Mom's concerts or reading books to Dad while he cooked. I decided that no kids in this school were ever going to find out that I played the violin, or that Mom … well, they weren't going to find out about her either. I had to think fast. Some cool but normal activity. "Um … you know, we just watched TV a lot on weekends, the usual stuff …"

"Like what shows?" asked Melissa.

As long as I can remember, we've never owned a

TV. I racked my brain for a show. "Sports!" I blurted out. "Hockey and … um … and … wrestling!"

"You like wrestling?" Tracy burst into a fit of giggles.

"C'mon, Trace," said Melissa, grabbing Tracy by her skinny arm. The others turned and followed.

They haven't said a word to me since, but I can tell they're whispering about me all the time. I can see them now in a clump at the edge of the soccer field, heading toward the school. It's just getting light, and everything is this eerie blue, but I can make out Tracy and Brianne sort of walking sideways so that they can still face Melissa and talk while they're walking. I slow down. If I walk slowly enough I'll get to the swing set just in time for the first bell. Then just before second bell I can slip into the classroom without anyone seeing me and miss sitting alone while they hover around Melissa's desk.

C'mon, bell, ring. There's this twist in my stomach. It's like before a performance—my heart's pounding and I know if I could throw up I'd feel better, but I can't. I feel stupid walking so slowly, so I swipe some new snow off the top of a crusty snowbank. It's like a big, blank sheet of paper, waiting. This weird feeling comes over me. All these kids are screaming in the playground, but it's as if they're in a glass bubble and I'm in this quiet space outside it. And I don't even care that the Town Girls have reached the monkey bars and might even be looking at me standing here alone. All I want to do is fill up this blank sheet of snow. I use a fist and the thumb of my mitt to make a sixteenth note, then three more and two eighths—the beginning of the Bach Double. I start to hum it. The bell rings and everyone's running in. I break into a run, still humming, step after step in time to the music, and open those double doors and walk right in.

⌣

Today is definitely my lucky day. Mrs. Friesen forgot to lock the library when she went for lunch. The rule at this school is that everyone goes outside for lunch, except on really cold days, like a blizzard or forty below. So on the first day in September I was on my way out to the playground but looking for an escape, and I passed the library and turned the handle just in case. No luck. I've turned the handle every day since, and it's always been locked. Mrs. Friesen is a very conscientious librarian.

I wonder what made her forget about it today? I can hear everyone out there screaming and throwing snowballs and sliding down the hill, and I bet

Melissa and Brianne and the rest are off in a corner comparing nail polish and talking about their dance routine. But in here ... it's dark and warm because I found a place right by the last shelf and the hot air vent. And I found a very old book with a hard brown cover about a British boarding school just for girls, and there's someone in it named Hilary who is the Head Girl and perfect in every way. She always has just the right thing to say. She's a genius at piano and field hockey and is nice to everyone, even Victoria, the jealous, nasty one who—

Click. Someone just came in. If it's Mrs. Friesen, and she needs to do some extra shelving and finds me back here ... I slowly tiptoe over to the next shelf and down the aisle. Someone is sitting at the piano. A very bald, very short, very hunched over man—Mr. Franckowiak, the custodian. What's he doing at the piano?

If there's one person who gets made fun of the most at Clear Lake Elementary School, even more than Josh, the scrawny kid with sticky-out ears in our Grade 6 class, it's Mr. Franckowiak. I guess it bugs everyone that he just minds his own business, pushes that old mop down the hallway, and never says a word, not even when Jeremy and some of the boys call him "Mr. Quack" and quack like ducks when he walks by and once knocked over his cleaning bucket on purpose after school and took off laughing before any of the teachers saw them. Mr. Franckowiak just mopped up the dirty water sloshing across the hallway. Then he picked up the empty bucket and walked down the hallway whistling a strange tune I'd never heard before. That big bunch of keys at his hip jangled and kind of went along with the tune, echoing down the empty hallway to the clang of his bucket.

He starts to play a fast dance. I've never heard it, but it makes me think of campfires and Gypsies kicking up their feet and the twirl of silk in a faraway place. I feel like dancing but I don't dare move a muscle, just grip the metal bookshelf a little harder.

He switches to something else—something steady and slow that I've heard before. I can't remember the name of it, but I know it's by Bach. I lean back against one of the shelves and sink down into the middle of a warm square of sun. The way he plays it—so steadily—helps me to breathe. It's like this morning at the edge of the playground—all those kids are screaming out there, but here it's so quiet and separate. He must really practise with his metronome because his rhythm is as solid as the book I'm holding. I trace my finger down its spine in time to the music …

The bell rings and he stops. Now if I can only get out of here without anyone seeing me. Mr. Franckowiak has disappeared. I quickly open the door and slip into the hallway streaming with kids. I don't think anyone saw me. I find myself behind Tracy and Melissa just ahead of Mr. Peters, our teacher.

While all the kids are getting out their books for Social Studies, Melissa turns around and whisper-hisses, "So where were you at lunch? We were looking for you."

I can't believe she's actually talking to me. The glimmer of her braces and tight smile make me go all topsy-turvy. "What did you want?" There. Nothing weird.

She flashes me her big braces smile and tosses back her hair. "Well … my mom told me it's not nice to … well … we had a little meeting this morning before school … Trace and Bri and I and … we decided …"

Mr. Peters is glaring at us. Melissa turns around quickly and starts scribbling in her notebook. He's writing stuff on the board and going on about the Riel Rebellion of 1885, some guy named Gabriel Dumont. What did Melissa and company decide? To dye their hair the same colour? A new move for their dance routine? Why would she want to tell me?

Mr. Peters goes to the cupboard and Melissa turns around again. "We've decided," she whispers, "that you can come over to my place after school. You can walk home with us. It's sort of a … test."

The topsy-turvy feeling explodes. "Test?!?" I shout out loud. Everyone turns around and stares. I lower my voice. "Why would I want to do that? I hate tests! They're"—I search for just the right word—"abominable!" People are starting to snicker. "Besides, I have to practise violin." I don't know what made me say all that. I slump my head into my arms.

"Hannah," says Mr. Peters, "while it's very fascinating indeed to hear your views on tests, I'd appreciate it if you would keep them to yourself during class. Both you and Melissa can stay after school and read the chapter on Gabriel Dumont."

"You just failed big time," whispers Melissa, turning her back to me.

Catharina

"Goodbye, Mama, goodbye, Lumpi!" Wilhelm and I stand on the street in front of our house and look up at her waving. "Will you sing us goodbye?" I say, stalling.

"Go on with you, Catharina! It's late!" Mama leans out the window. "Mind you get Wilhelm to his school on time!" I don't see why I still must walk Wilhelm to the Latin school. The law doesn't require me to stay at school past my eleventh year, so I finished at the St. Agnus School last spring. Yet Papa and Mama still insist that I continue to walk with Wilhelm. Perhaps today, after I return, Mama will take a break from her chores and we'll sit in the kitchen and have a warm roll and coffee and sing.

I clutch Wilhelm's hand, look back at her still waving in the window. She'll stay until we've turned the corner onto Magdeburger Street.

"Ewww!" Wilhelm is laughing and pointing down to the cobblestones, to my new shiny black shoe with the little heel. "You've gone and stepped in horse poop!" He holds his nose.

I look down. Sure enough, there's a soft, brown lump on the pointed toe and a bit of it on my satin overskirt as well. Now what will I do? We can't go back home or we'll be terribly late.

"Ewww! I have to get away from the stink!" Wilhelm, still holding his nose, twists away from my hand and runs ahead.

The rascal! I lift my skirts and run as best as I can with the corset pinching my chest every step of the way. I see the ringlets of his white wig bob into the alley, the shortcut to the town square. Ha! I'll go the other way round and cut him off at Frau Fischer's asparagus stall! Faster, under a clothesline and the slap of a wet shirt in my face, past the old man out smoking his pipe, into the market! I am sweating under these layers of dresses in the hot sun. Faster! Spilled asparagus!

"Frau Fischer, I'm so sorry—"

She's frowning down at her precious bunches of white asparagus on the cobblestones. I bend to pick them up.

"Never mind." Her face is kind. She takes my arm and points to the next stall. "Your brother!"

I can see his satin coat peeking from behind a loaf of bread in the next stall. I race around the other side and catch his hand. He holds his nose again.

I grab his lacy collar. "Wait until I tell Mama!"

He's grinning from ear to ear. "Then I'll tell Papa and everyone all about you and the poop! Ewww!"

As we near the Latin school, a chorus of boys— Wilhelm's mean friends—chant my name in four-part harmony. "Speak up!" "Say something for once, girl!" they yell as we draw closer.

Worms! I want to yell, but all I can manage is to open my mouth and shut it, feel my face go hot. Wilhelm lets go of my hand again and runs to join them. I hurry away. Now he'll tell them everything and I will never hear the end of it—tomorrow's chant will most likely have something about poop in it.

I keep running until I'm under the shade of the linden right next to our house, under the bear statues that sit above the door of our St. Agnus Lutheran Church. I'm shaking and panting, sweating like a horse. Why did I inherit such a rascal for a brother? And Carl will only follow in his footsteps, and then Johann. Will I always have to walk them to school, year after year?

I sit down on a bench and try to clean my shoe with a leaf. "It's a waste of time for me to walk Wilhelm to school. I'd rather … attend the Latin school myself!" I'd say to Papa with the boldest voice. No, not my voice, but I can hear it distinctly … it seems strange, but I think it belongs to the girl, that small one I saw before falling asleep the other night. When Papa looks at her, shocked and angry for being impertinent, she just carries on. "It seems to me very unfair that only boys can attend the Latin school. After all, I'm quite competent in Latin." Then, to Papa's utter amazement, she starts listing off verbs, the ones I've memorized from Wilhelm's grammar text! "*Abnuo, acuo, arguo, delibuo, exuo, imbuo,*" she says, trying to keep from giggling at Papa's shocked expression. Then she really starts having fun, reciting Martial's funny little poem about the big nose: "*'Tongilianus habet nasum: scio, non nego: sed iam Nil praeter nasum Tongilianus habet,'*" followed by its translation. "Tongilianus has a nose: I know that, I don't deny that. But at present time, he has nothing except a nose."

I laugh out loud. If only this girl existed! I'd most certainly take lessons in speaking to Papa from her! I sigh and look back at the way I've come, where the Latin school *does* exist, without any girls in it and with a nasty little brother who will need picking up by the end of the day. The hem of my skirt is still stained with poop. I furiously try to rub it off. What will I tell Mama? And what if Wilhelm tattles about this morning's chase to Papa?

⌒

Mama is too busy to notice my dirty hem, because Tante Lena is sick again. Well, probably not really sick, just too tired to leave her bed.

"Take this tray up to her room," says Mama with a wink. "I'm sure the apple strudel will have her

34

down here singing with us by afternoon coffee."

"Will there really be a chance to sing this afternoon?" I ask, looking back before I reach the stairs.

She sprinkles flour onto a board. "Perhaps ... but first I must finish this baking, and you must do the sweeping, and then to market, and then the roast—"

"And then it will be time for me to pick up Wilhelm again."

"And what about your assignment?" Even though I no longer attend school, Mama insists that I keep up my penmanship and sums with a small assignment each day. "How about, when you're finished with that tray and with the sweeping, a letter, in your best hand, to one of your relatives? We can send it with the mail coach the day after tomorrow."

"Yes, Mama." I trudge up the stairs and think about whom to write. Uncle Johann Bach in Erfurt? Cousin Christoph Bach in Ohrdruf? Tante Elisabeth Bach in Arnstadt? I have enough Bach uncles and aunts and cousins to require a whole forest of paper because Mama was also a Bach before she married Papa. Her father was a Bach who died before I was born, and he was a great composer and organist, just like Papa. The Bachs are all great musicians. Greatness runs in our blood.

Well, in everyone's but mine. Now I've done it—spilled coffee on Tante Lena's tray. She frowns in disapproval, and I make my escape before she can say anything. All during the sweeping—from Papa's rehearsal chamber down to the landing at the bottom of the stairs—I think about whom to write. But even when I'm sitting at the table at the back of the pantry under the hanging braids of garlic with a blank sheet of paper and a quill and a pot of ink, I still haven't decided. "Really, Catharina, it shouldn't be so hard," I tell myself. "Tante Elisabeth would love to receive a letter."

What if, just for fun, I write a letter to the girl? I'm not sure where she lives—not tiresome old Cöthen or Erfurt but some distant land that would take years by carriage to reach. I take a quill and begin.

May 14, 1720

Dear Girl,

But I'm stuck. What should I write? *Today I swept the floor and walked my brother to school.* She would think me incredibly dull and never write back. Two flies buzz in from the window and land on my shoe, on the traces of dung I couldn't get off, then circle up high to the ceiling like two black eighth notes— ♫ —two eighth notes! Two melodies! *The* concerto … the one I heard Papa play that night, the one for two solo violins—that's what I'll write!

I dip the pen in ink. A sixteenth note. Then three more and two eighths. I try a little flourish on the tail of the eighth, just like Mama. Ha! They think I know nothing. I copy the whole line just as I remember from seeing the music Mama copied by the river that day. I hum the melody under my breath as I write the letter beneath the music.

I'm sorry, I haven't figured out a name for you yet. I hope you like the music I copied above. My papa composed it. This is the part for the second violin. I love listening to him play it on his new violin—like a dance, with lively strokes of the bow, and great emphasis on the rhythm, which I think is most important in this movement.

I very much admired how you spoke to Papa this morning. How could you speak to him like that? I would never have the courage. I'd appreciate you telling me sometime how you did it. The poem about the nose was funny, too.

In the meantime, I must sign off, because there are a million tasks to do to help my mama, and then unfortunately, I must walk to the Latin school again to pick up my rascal of a brother. Do you have brothers? I have three.

Respectfully yours,
Catharina Dorthea Bach

P.S. I love to sing. What do you love to do?

Three

Catharina

I'M WALKING AS A STATELY LADY would. Well, walking in as stately a manner as she might with traces of horse dung on her shoes, on the way to pick up her little brother, while awaiting a chorus of his friends singing in four parts a terrible rendition of her name.

My heart races as I reach the Latin school, and I stall by burying my nose in the lilac hedge that surrounds it. These are Mama's favourite. Two years ago at this very time of year, when Papa travelled to Berlin to purchase a harpsichord for the prince and was gone for a month, Herr Colm, the copyist, came over with a big bunch of lilacs. I answered the door.

"These are for your mama," he said, looking down at the street with a red face. "Your papa asked me to collect them and bring them to her in his absence."

Then he hurried into his carriage and rode away.

"From Johann!" Mama said, and her face lit up at the sight of them. The whole house smelled of lilac for the next two days, and I kept catching Mama with her nose in them. By the dreamy look on her face, I could tell she was thinking about Papa, trying to be patient and wait until the day he would walk through that door.

I wish I could pick these for her! But the Latin school headmaster would most likely catch me. I peek out from behind the lilacs, expecting the chorus of boys, but there's only Wilhelm.

"What's wrong?" I ask as I approach. He wears the most dejected expression.

"The boys …"

I can tell by the way he's twitching his mouth and shuffling his feet over the grass that he's about to cry. "Did they run away?"

He nods. "They called me a name …"

"You too? Well, then there's a pair of us." I'm forgetting about his impertinence this morning. After all, he *is* only nine. And those boys! Wait until Mama hears about it! Better yet— I'll gather up the courage to tell Papa, who'll tell the headmaster, who will in turn serve them a beating!

"Listen," I say in my gentlest voice. "Why don't

we take a walk through the palace grounds before going home?"

His mouth stops twitching. "We'll enter by the stables and take a look at the horses," I carry on, "then on to that pretty water garden in the shape of a star, and on to Prince Leopold's Orangery, maybe even the Deer Garden—"

"Oh, Cathe, do you think we could even—"

"Sneak by the Ludwigsbau for a listen to Papa's music? Of course."

His face is lit up with excitement, like Mama with the lilacs. He takes a deep breath. I know what's coming. "Do you think we could try ... the Little Maze?" Then he adds, pointing to my shoe, "I won't say a thing to Papa about the you-know-what."

I break into laughter. Me, tripping in all my big skirts through the marketplace with poop on my shoe! Papa must never hear of it. Wilhelm has been pestering me to take him through the maze for months. And even though I'm frightened of it, I've really been longing to try, ever since I heard the prince bragging at a concert that it's the only one of its kind in all of Anhalt! Mama keeps promising to take us through after a concert, but then it's always too late. And I really should ask for permission first, but ...

"This once," I say, grabbing his hand. We race off to the palace.

It's a very warm day, and all the gardeners are out clipping the hedges into perfect rectangles. I run my hand along a hedge as we pass, and wish for something softer. Sometimes I grow tired of one square garden after the next, of all these little green globes and perfect shapes. Wilhelm tugs my hand and I try to slow him down. "We must walk ever so slowly to preserve our strength for the maze," I say, trying to speak like Her Highness Mother the Princess Agnes.

We pass the stables and wave to the stable master and feed the last of Wilhelm's lunch to the prince's white stallions. We pass Herr Rose in the fencing field, teaching his class of young pages. They face him with their foils by their sides. He glances over and sees us. "Now, in pairs—parry in *six* and riposte in *quatre*!" he instructs, then walks over to us.

He wipes the sweat from his forehead. "And how are the children of Johann Sebastian this fine May day?"

"Fine, Herr Rose," says Wilhelm. "But why aren't you playing in the concert?"

"Your papa has no need of an oboe in this week's concerto! Leaves me more time for fencing. And believe me, these young fellows need it!" He turns around to observe his pupils, then faces us again. "You both should hear the concert!" He looks at his pocket watch. "You'll just catch the end of it. I heard the rehearsal yesterday. Such music! Your papa's finest work to date!"

I wonder if he means *the* piece, the Concerto for Two Violins. I simply must hear it. I grab Wilhelm's hand and we wave goodbye to Herr Rose. To the Ludwigsbau, for music!

Wilhelm tugs my hand. "The maze, the Little Maze—"

"Of course, but music first. You heard what Herr Rose said. Papa's finest work to date!" I hurry past the Star Garden with all its horse fountains, think of the stars that night when I listened to Papa compose the piece.

It seems to take us ages to reach the Ludwigsbau. I can already hear the music spilling through the windows as we cross the bridge over the moat and approach the grand gate with the soldiers on either side. The concert must be in the Spiegelsaal, the Hall of Mirrors.

"Let's just sit on this bench in the courtyard and listen," says Wilhelm, as we pass the guards who give us a nod and a wink that make me blush. "Then we'll have more time to get to the maze."

I don't mind just listening from outside. I knew as soon as we passed the grand gate that they weren't playing the piece. It's another piece for orchestra and voice; the prince must have hired a soprano. They finish the movement and a slow movement begins—a duet for violin and voice. The violin ... I can tell it's not Herr Spiess but ... Papa ... playing the duet on his new violin! I heard him practising it last night. What is it about the sound of this violin and the voice? I close my eyes and listen as hard as I can—it's like looking into a deep well and watching a stone fall through the reflections on the surface, watching it swirl down, down into the deep black water. I pretend that it's my voice swirling along with Papa's violin, that I'm up there in the concert hall, making music with Papa for the prince.

"The maze!" Wilhelm is impatient, and I realize the applause has already sounded. The guards turn at his voice and laugh and talk among themselves. Snooty old guards! What do you know about it? Wilhelm grabs my hand and we run off.

The Little Maze isn't far away, back over the moat bridge on the other side, through some more gardens and into the very corner of the palace grounds. In the centre are a miniature gazebo and a pond. Mama says the maze is absolutely charming, and I've been longing to see it. The trick is to find your way around the rows and rows of tall hedges and dead ends. We find the entrance easily enough. It's so quiet, just the chirp of a few birds. All the gardeners must be working near the stables. I take a deep breath and step in, surrounded by the high green walls.

"Make a left here!" Wilhelm has run ahead, and I can barely see his white wig bob before he disappears around the corner.

I think about this morning's escapade. "Don't run too far ahead! We must stay—" But it's too late. I pick up my skirts and run, make a left, and see him already turning another corner. I run faster and catch him by the coat. "We must stay together. Otherwise we're in trouble."

He's jumping up and down with excitement. "That way!" He points to a hedge. "No, maybe over there!" He points to another one, identically green. "Oh, how are we supposed to know which way to take?"

"Shh!" I stand very still. Surely there must be a clue, something other than these rows and rows of trimmed green. I remember Mama saying something about a miniature fountain by the gazebo. Fountains make a sound, so when we're close enough to the centre, we'll hear it. I close my eyes and listen with all my might. Nothing. I calmly lead the way around a curved hedge that's like the curve of Mama's cheek— it somehow has more purpose than all the square hedges. We follow it for quite a while.

"Do you smell something?" I ask, stopping again.

He shakes his head. He's sunburned, and kicks at the carpet-like grass. All his enthusiasm seems to have worn off.

"Smell harder! I think it's … is it lilac?" Perhaps there's a hedge by the gazebo! Only Mama didn't mention it because she wasn't there when it was blooming. I make a turn toward where I think the scent is coming from, and Wilhelm follows. I stop and close my eyes and listen again, listen hard, like the nights I listen to Papa compose. Is it a trickle, like water in a brook? Yes! The fountain. Now we just need to follow the sound to the centre.

"Come, we're almost there!" I shout and pull him around a corner, then into a dead end and back, then another turn, following the sound of the fountain and the smell of Mama's favourite flower.

"The gazebo!" Wilhelm shouts and runs inside. It's so small that there's barely enough room for the two of us. I run my hand over the bench's cool marble. Everything is silent, as if the gazebo holds a spell. There are mirrors, too, so that wherever I look

I see another me with a bunch of lilacs behind my head. I rest my cheek against a marble pillar and gaze at one of the mirrors.

"Hello!" I say to myself. "Did you like the maze?" I wiggle my nose and brush some hair away from my forehead.

"You're silly, Catharina, talking to yourself in the mirror!" Wilhelm says and runs off to the miniature pond.

I don't care what he thinks. This is one of my favourite games; I've played it before with mirrors in the palace, talking to myself as if I'm really another person. I watch a small trickle of sweat run down my cheek—I mean the cheek of the girl in the mirror. "Are you very hot and tired?"

She nods.

"Never mind. When you get home, your mama will have a nice supper all waiting for you. Do you think so?"

She's very still, as if something terrible has happened, and I feel an ache for no reason at all—this has never happened before in any of my mirror games. A cloud has drifted over the sun. I shiver with goosebumps as the mirror darkens. The girl staring back is me ... but not me, somehow. Perhaps she's the girl, trying to answer my letter?

Her nose *does* look bigger, her eyes look darker, and for some reason, the ache feels as if it could turn to crying. I close my eyes to blink away the tears.

When I open them the sun is shining again. I look in the mirror, and of course it's just me after all—it must have been a trick of the weather. It's still just my game, and I must think of something that will make the girl feel better. "Lilacs are my mama's favourite. She … is the most beautiful woman in the world—no … don't worry, I don't look anything like her. She has the longest, thickest blond hair to her waist, and her voice—"

Mama! I glance up at the sun. It's getting late. She and Tante Lena will be frantic making preparations for Papa's arrival at home. And if he beats us there!

"Let's go," I call out to Wilhelm. "Mama will be so worried!" I take one more glance in the mirror. I'm just as sunburned as Wilhelm. And Mama will scold me for forgetting my cap at home. I hate to leave, but take Wilhelm's hand firmly in my own. "Goodbye!" I wave to myself in the mirror and we start back into the maze at a run.

Getting out is ten times harder than going in, without the smell of lilac and the sound of the fountain to guide me, and with Wilhelm dawdling behind and whining. And it was his idea in the first place! Green, green, all I can see is green, and one opening looks just like the next. We keep running into dead ends, and I get the feeling that we're running in circles. I smell the lilac again, just when I want away from it.

"Please, let's rest? I'm thirsty." Wilhelm has stopped and plopped himself down in the half shade of a circular dead-end hedge. I try not to cry and stand beside him; I can't risk getting grass stains on my skirt. What sounds lie outside of the maze? Herr Felici, the Italian gardener singing songs of his homeland with his deep voice? No, he'll surely be off tending to the prince's precious orange trees. Surely there's a way I can listen our way out of this puzzle. And then I hear it ... so far away and faint, but I'm sure of it, drifting all the way through these horrible hedges, straight to me. *The* piece.

"Wilhelm, do you hear it? Papa's music?"

He shakes his head and slowly stands up, takes my hand. His eyes seem glazed over. He's had too much sun.

"Come, hurry, I can find the way out!" Someone is playing the second violin part of the Concerto for Two Violins. I sing the first part to go with it, and loop around these hedges as if I'm the melody and the hedges are the lines of the staff. I listen again, and run through another few openings, under, over … I laugh, and run in time to the music, singing as we go.

"Catharina!" Wilhelm pants after me. "I've never heard you sing like that before." We slow down a bit to catch our breath. "Where did you learn it?" He looks at me with suspicion.

"I told you—it's Papa's music, his double violin concerto, and it's not really so hard to sing, even while running through a maze!" I begin to run and pull him after me. "Come, we're almost there!" I could almost leap over the dead ends! Ha! We reach the opening entrance, and I expect Papa to be standing there, putting the flourish on the final note of the first movement.

No Papa. It's so silent—just a few birds chirping their evening song.

"What happened to the music?" I let go of Wilhelm's hand. "His concerto … it was just here … so clear … it led us out of the maze!"

Wilhelm looks at me as if I'm mad as old Salome from down the lane. "Talking to yourself in the mirror, singing *da-da-da-da dee-dee* through the maze, and now … hearing music where there is none! I won't tell Papa any of it! He'll be too worried about you—silly Catharina!" He turns away from me. "Papa! Papa!"

Papa is walking toward us. I can tell from his quick gait that he's worried. Wilhelm runs ahead and throws himself into Papa's arms. "We found the tiny gazebo by listening to the fountain, and found the way out by—"

"We were very worried." Papa scowls and looks straight at me, and I feel my tongue freeze up in spite of the warm weather. Oh, speak! You stupid! Why can't you speak? I was all ready after hearing the music and now I'm mute as a rabbit.

Wilhelm is dancing circles around Papa. "Papa, there were lilacs at the gazebo, just perfect for Mama, and a mirror, and lovely, cool marble—"

"Yes, yes, my boy, it is all wonderful. But what if you hadn't been able to find your way out? The guards informed me you were heading for the Little Maze, and so I quickly came here to look." He glares at me. Again I can't speak. "As the eldest, you should have received permission from me or Mama first before attempting such an adventure. This is a warning. Know better next time."

And now I will cry. But I musn't cry, not in front of Papa. "Never mind now." He picks up his violin case and takes Wilhelm's hand. "Mama and Tante Lena will have supper waiting for us, and I have some special news. Come now, children. It'll only take us a few minutes if we walk quickly."

I follow along behind and try to keep from crying. I mustn't, mustn't … Then I see Papa's violin case. It must have been Papa—who else? But why didn't he say anything about playing? Then again, it didn't sound like Papa's new violin—the music was clear but less … less in tune than what he would play, less like the deep black water in the well. Tonight … after supper, I'll ask him. I'll lift my head and say, "Papa, that was you playing the double concerto to lead us out of the maze, wasn't it?" And then I'll go on to tell about Wilhelm's friends and suggest he have a talk with the headmaster. And Papa will smile and put his hand on my shoulder and say, "Catharina, how clever you are, a true Bach. And so brave, to hear the music and lead your brother out of that difficult maze."

I practise lifting my head to look at the back of Papa's wig. The girl would always be able to face her papa. She'd look him straight in the eye.

Hannah

"How would you like to play your violin in a school assembly?" asks Ms. Lockport as we near the city.

She's the secretary at our school but lives in the city and so I catch rides with her every Monday. A whole week since my last lesson and I've practised every day. I played through the whole thing last night with only one slip, almost all from memory. Just wait until Mr. Dekker hears it.

Ms. Lockport glances at me expectantly. Play at a school assembly? I'd rather listen to a hundred organ concerts. Ever since the disaster with Melissa in Social Studies, she's managed to tell everyone in the school that I play the violin. It's normal at our school to play the piano and recorder, but I'm the only kid in the whole town who plays the violin. And now I won't hear the end of it. On Friday, Jeremy and Ben came up to me at recess in violin positions making squawking noises. You'd think the violin was some instrument from ancient Egypt, the way everyone's going on.

"Um … I'll have to think about it and talk to Mr. Dekker and my dad first." I make a small port-hole with my fingertip against the window frost. "Like, you know, to see if I have time to prepare adequately and stuff—we're getting horrendous heaps of homework these days."

"I just thought it would be nice for the other kids to see what you do," she says, shifting the gears.

"Um … right." I give a sigh of relief as we pull into Mr. Dekker's driveway. "Thanks a lot, Ms. Lockport," I say quickly and make my escape. I let myself in the back door and ignore the sign above the boot rack: "NO CLAWS ALLOWED! (Except Penny)." A pair of nail clippers is duct-taped to the sign on the end of a string. I glance down at my nails—perfectly trimmed. I cut them before my practice last night. Nothing's going to get in the way of today's triumph.

Bridget is still in her lesson, so I check to see if there's a new painting above Penny's dish—it's still *Starry Night*—then settle into the squishy couch in the living room and look out the window. It's started to snow. Part of me wants to head straight for the bookshelves and find something about gnomes or zoos to read, but another part of me can't stop watching the snow. It's really falling thickly—flakes and flakes covering everything, making it all quiet. The only sound is Mr. Dekker and Bridget playing … the Bach Double, but they've finished the first movement and have moved on to the slow movement, the one played at Mom's funeral.

The snowflakes and the music swirl around in time together—slowly drifting up and down, erasing all the traffic and city sounds. I drift with the snowflakes and the music back to that day when I sat in the cathedral listening to this with the awful, gaping hole where Mom had been. That day and the next and for months afterwards, I kept trying to fill up the hole by imagining pictures of her—Mom on a bright fall day at Kensington Market inspecting a pile of red peppers that matched her scarf, Mom with her violin-case backpack leading the way through a crowd at the station, the contented look she had when we played our scales together so in tune that we sounded like one violin. "Listen for the ringing tones that match your open strings," she'd say. "Listen ..."

And the time she tried to teach me to dance the minuet. "*One*, two, three," she said, holding my hand in promenade position as we practised the step in her studio, around and around until I began to get the feel of it. "Imagine the way people would have looked and moved back then," she said. "Women in elegant dresses over layers of petticoats, the bowing and the curtsying and the little flourishes people made with their hands." Her hand swept down to the floor in little curlicues as she made a grand bow. I tried to copy her and giggled and lost my balance.

When I straighten up to take her outstretched hand, it's smaller ... the hand of a girl who seems about my age, but she's lucky to have a much smaller nose. She seems big for her age, though, big-boned and tall, the kind of girl who could play forward on the basketball team or get picked first for softball, unlike scrawny little me. "Care to dance?" she asks so softly that I can hardly hear. "My dancing master said I'm hopeless at the minuet, but—"

"Oh, please, yes! I've played a million minuets on the violin, but I'd love to learn the dance. Can you teach me?"

"I'll try," she says, lifting my hand to begin. "Just watch my feet." After concentrating hard on the steps and skips of her shiny black shoes for a while, I look up and realize there's a crowd of other people dancing, too—women in fancy satin gowns and men in funny pants that reach only to the knees, everyone wearing wigs, candles fixed in holders along the walls and in huge chandeliers, a long, velvet couch along the wall, and up in the balcony, a real orchestra playing one of the minuets by Bach.

"Is this your first noble ball?" she asks, as we near the balcony.

I nod. "I wish it would go on forever!" I say, falling into the rhythm of the dance and feeling as if I'm floating on a breeze of colour and sound. We move near to the balcony and something catches my eye—the wood of one of the violins. I crane my neck to see. Even from a distance it glints in the candlelight and reminds me of ... it's, it's ... I forget all about my feet and they get tangled up. I back into a man and trip, sprawling down to the hardwood floor.

"Hannah, are you COMPLETELY CRAZY?" Bridget's sharp voice looms above me and I realize that I'm sitting in the middle of Mr. Dekker's floor with my arms outstretched and a few books knocked off the coffee table. "What are you DOING?"

"Um ..." I stand and push up my glasses. "I was just practising the steps to the minuet." Was I actually just dancing at a ball? And I think I saw Mom's violin, up in the balcony—in fact, I'm almost sure of it. It was all so real—the music is still floating somewhere above me.

"What a good idea," says Mr. Dekker, smiling in the doorway to the studio, "to use the time while Bridget and I were reviewing the Bach minuets to practise the rhythm by dancing. You know that it actually is a dance?"

I nod. "Mom tried to teach it to me once."

A sleek grey sports car has pulled up in the driveway. Bridget's mom honks the horn, and Bridget looks at her watch. "I have to get to ballet.

Bye, Mr. Dekker!" she calls out. "I'll have the Handel memorized by next week for sure!"

The Handel. I push up my glasses. Bridget is well into Book 6, probably almost in 7. Plus she's a year younger than me. She's only playing the Bach Double part at the end of Book 5 and the minuets from Book 1 for review. That floating feeling I had dancing at the ball with the girl slips away, replaced by a twisty feeling in my stomach as I watch Bridget with her blond ponytail bob into the car.

I give my violin handle a squeeze and follow Mr. Dekker into the studio. If only I could really show him for once how much I practised.

"Nice intonation," says Mr. Dekker after I've played my G major three-octave scale. All my hard work paid off—wait until I tell Dad. "Now, the Bach. This piece is all about listening. It's like a conversation between two people. Here—" He plays my opening solo. "Then when I come in with my answer, you hold back a little to give me room to speak. Then it's back and forth, back and forth—sometimes you're moving up while I'm moving down, we move apart and then come back together again. But, just as in a conversation, if you listen well enough, you can't get lost." He puts his violin into playing position. "We're off!"

"But ... but I have to play the whole thing for you first alone before I'm allowed ..."

He just waits with his violin up and ready to go. There's nothing for me to do but start. I take a deep breath. The beginning's easy enough. Steady, steady ... listen! There he is, starting just the way I did, and I quiet down a little to hear him. Now we have these short bits back and forth—he holds a half note, as if he's thinking while I speak, then it switches around. Here I'm the main speaker again and now ... listen ... yes, he answers back, only higher up. Ha! I bet even Bridget the Perfect can't play as well as this! And what if Melissa and company could see me ... and Mom ... if she could see me now ... but where *am* I now? I was supposed to shift here but ... I'm lost, I can't find what I need to say; the notes aren't here. Dead end. What happened? I practised so hard and I *was* getting it.

"... the best ..." Mr. Dekker's voice is muffled, as if it's coming in from a different planet. What's he saying? Something about it being the best I've ever played. It can't be. I must be hearing wrong. "And next week you'll play it all through."

Right. I look at myself in the mirror. My reflection's getting all blurry. No, I can't cry, I won't. Not in my lesson.

"… Aunt Rhody, in third position, with your best tone. I'll play the duet part. Listen …"

"Go Tell Aunt Rhody"! Back to Book 1. I won't tell Dad. I lift up my violin to play and try to look at Mr. Dekker for the upbeat and at my reflection in the mirror, but I'm just a blurry mass in a faraway land.

Four

Hannah

"YOU OKAY?" Ms. Dumont fiddles with a switch and glances back at me. I have a seat to myself, right at the front. It's pretty quiet, just the swish of the wipers against the snow, the rustle of Peppermint Woman's peppermints.

"Fine." I guess she noticed me scrunching my face against the window instead of doing homework. I have my book open but I can't read a word.

"You sure?" she says. I just nod and pretend to study.

"What's for homework?"

"The Riel Rebellion. We have a test tomorrow."

"Gabriel Dumont?"

"Yup." I could show her the picture in my textbook of Dumont in a plaid shirt and plaid pants with one arm around a horse and another holding a gun, but all I want to do is stare out at the fields.

I think she can tell, because she starts humming a tune in time with the wipers.

Swish, swish. The Bach Double would fit into the wipers' rhythm, too, but I never want to hear that piece again. How will I manage that? I have to master it before moving on to Book 5. I could beg Mr. Dekker to let me skip it. He'd never. Besides, how long have I been waiting to play it?

Since Mom first played it at my lesson. "I want to quit," I said. My usual threat. She didn't even look surprised or say anything, not that I was expecting her to. I figured she'd just start some crazy game or duet and we'd end up traipsing through the house on our knees playing "Rhody Goes to Cairo" and I'd end up giggling and saying, "There's no way I'll ever quit" like always. But when she lifted her violin to her chin, and her mouth twisted in concentration, I knew this was something different. It was like her music was on fire … leaping and dancing and calling me to join in. After she finished, she said, "We'll play it together someday."

"Right, Mom," I whisper to the fields. How can they be so empty? In Toronto, there were people, people, always people and buildings and noise filling everything up, and cars honking and sirens going that day in the hospital when I stood by her bed. "I'll never quit, I promise," I said, handing her a purple crocus I'd picked from the back hospital lawn when I thought no one was watching. Every spring, Mom and I had a contest to see who could spot the first crocus. She usually won, except that year.

But I could quit. Then I'd never have to hear the Bach Double again, played by me, Bridget the Perfect, or anyone else. I'd walk home with Melissa and Tracy and Brianne every day and go to Melissa's and work on their dance routine, and Jeremy and Ben would leave me alone, and I wouldn't have to play at the school assembly. "You'd understand, wouldn't you, Mom?" I whisper again to the tiny lights of some distant farm that are like earrings in my reflection in the window. And then it's like my reflection with the farm-light earrings whispers back, "Quit? How could you think of such a thing? *Quitting isn't an option. Practise only on the days that you eat!*" These were two signs that Mom had posted on the door to her studio. She meant it, too. All her students, including me, practised every day no matter what.

"Gabriel Dumont was my grandfather's grandfather. That would make him my great-great-grandfather," says a voice from far away. I jerk away from my reflection. It's Ms. Dumont. What's she saying about her grandfather? She's related to Gabriel Dumont?

"Really?" I glance down at my textbook and then at her. "I have his picture—see?" I bring my book up to show her.

"Yup," she says, glancing down. "Grandpa has the original framed on his wall. It's a lot bigger."

"Your grandfather's still alive?"

"We're going to celebrate his ninety-second birthday. Pretty old, eh? It's going to be a great time—we'll all be fiddling and dancing, even Grandpa Joe! He says it's the music that's keeping him alive—"

"I play the fiddle ... um ... I mean, the violin." I reach up to the rack and grab my case, get it down without knocking it against anything. Peppermint Woman's got her eye on me.

"I've noticed you carrying that in and out of here every Monday." Ms. Dumont glances down. "Your case is a little fancier than mine. Mine's a bit beat up—my uncle gave it to me."

"You play the fiddle too?"

"Sure ... you ever hear the tune 'Whiskey before Breakfast'?"

I shake my head.

"How about 'Big John McNeil'? 'St. Anne's Reel'? 'Growlin' Old Man and Woman'?"

I shake my head again. "I don't know any fiddle. I've always just played classical stuff."

"Oh! You've got to learn these! They're too much fun." She turns to me and smiles and her eyes are so clear, and blue as the snow when I'm walking to school. "How about … you come to the party? I could teach you a tune or two and you could meet some of the family … little Billy and Aunt Bernadette, she makes the best Saskatoon pie for miles around, and Grandpa Joe and Uncle Maurice—they'd all love to meet you."

I twist my strap. "I'd have to ask my dad first—"

"Sure! Better yet, why don't you bring your mom and dad along? There'll be lots of fiddle and dance and pie!"

"My mom …" There's something about her that makes me want to tell. "My mom's … dead."

"I'm sorry." She's silent for a while and I feel kind of dumb, so I just sit back down in my seat. "You could bring along your dad. You told me before that you just moved … I'll bet he gets kind of lonely after living in … where did you say you lived before?"

"Toronto."

"I'll bet he'd just love a party."

Party? She doesn't know Dad since … since Mom died. I wrap my arms around my violin. "Sure, I'll ask anyway."

"Grandpa's birthday is a week from this Saturday. I'll write out my phone number for you just as soon as we stop in Clear Lake. Oh, you'll like 'St. Anne's Reel.' It's my favourite."

"I'll ask my dad as soon as I get home. Thanks … thanks a lot, Ms. Dumont."

"Call me Marie." She turns the bus into town.

"Thanks … Marie." I close all my books and look back at the window. Fiddle lessons and a party with Gabriel Dumont's great-great-granddaughter! The girl in the window has changed earrings—now she's wearing the lights of town. "Quit? How could you ever think of such a thing?" She smiles and hugs her violin.

"But, Dad, it will be an educational experience! Maybe I can interview Marie's grandpa for a report or something!"

He slowly winds the last of his spaghetti around his fork. "I don't know these people. They could … kidnap you."

"Oh, Dad. No one kidnaps anyone in Clear Lake! And besides, you'll be there. Marie invited you, too."

He quietly places his fork on his plate. The spaghetti he's left looks forlorn. "I have to finish the floor. And get the wiring done and that drywall before we freeze—"

"But … but you never go out, except downtown to get groceries, and … and you must get so sick of being in this old house all the time, in here just renovating and reading all the time and—"

"That's enough, Hannah." His chair scraping the bare floor makes me shiver. I can tell by the edge to his voice that he won't say any more. He pulls a thick book from the shelf and leaves the kitchen. And then, after his slow trudge up the stairs, I hear the door to his room quietly closing. Is he taking out her violin? Is he looking at it and remembering all the parties at our house in Toronto? People would come over with their instruments—Renée and Claire with their violins, sometimes other people from the symphony with cellos and violas. And there was Joseph with his guitar and Michael who played our piano. Dad sat in his big chair taking it all in and smiling, as if there was no other place he'd rather be than sitting in the midst of all of that music. Mom was in the centre of it all, her violin glinting in the candlelight. I played too, just playing open strings before I could read music, and then when I could read, she wrote out easy parts for me.

"Just a little longer?" I always asked, even though I knew it was no use. But even going to bed was okay, because I listened to them play late into the night, the notes from Mom's violin drifting up to me like smoke. I think she spent more time with her violin under her chin than doing anything else. It must be lonely in its case all the time—under Dad's bed? In a closet somewhere?

I run the water for the dishes. It's the only noise in the house, except for the creaks and the cracks, and the old kitchen clock, tick-tocking the time away. Tick tock tick tock. Like a metronome, calling me to play. I can't stand this silence. I leave the spaghetti pot in the dishwater to soak and race up the stairs, straight to my violin.

I play facing the window and the stars and the half moon. I have to fill up this house. *We'll play it together someday.* I imagine the first violin part winding around the notes I'm playing. I can hear it so clearly. It's as if … I'm singing it … but it's not my voice. I close my eyes and listen as I play. Is it the girl singing, the one from the ball? There's so much energy in her voice, and freedom, the notes running up high, then down again, leaping up and catching a quick breath before jumping in again. It feels like laughing. I shift to that high D over on the E string and give it a bit of vibrato, even though it's my fourth finger and that's the hardest. And then it's as if I'm running with her all the way to the end, when we land on the final note together.

I stop playing. It's silent, except for my panting, as if I've just been running and singing, too. There's sweat on my fingerboard and my hand with the bow is shaking. For the first time, I've just made it all the way through the second violin part of the first movement of the Concerto for Two Violins by Johann Sebastian Bach from memory without a stop. Whose voice helped me to play that way? I look at my reflection in the window. Of course it's me ... but not me ... she's tall, taller than the grain elevator, so tall that the half moon is her earring. She's holding up her violin in victory.

Catharina

"No, Wilhelm. We'll have no announcements until you've finished your asparagus." Mama's voice is stern. "You must be hungry after traipsing around the Little Maze all afternoon."

"I hate asparagus. It's white and thin and spooky … like ghost fingers!" Wilhelm rattles his knife and fork down on his plate and wiggles his fingers, gives Carl a poke. Carl starts to cry.

"Ghosts!" Tante Lena curls her long, thin fingers around her knife. "Talk of ghosts at the dinner table. I never heard of such a thing." She cuts her ham. She looks like a ghost, so white and frail. Tante Lena is much older than Mama and has lived with us for as long as I can remember. She's forever disapproving of things and going to her room for a rest.

Johann has begun to cry along with Carl. He's only a year younger and copies everything that Carl does.

"Wilhelm, now look at what you've started—" Mama begins. Wilhelm has the hiccups and begins to giggle.

"Quiet, everyone!" Papa stands and raps his knuckles on the table in a complicated rhythm, as if he's calling the court *capelle* to order. Everyone immediately follows his orders and sits perfectly still, even Lumpi, who's been brushing against my leg for scraps.

Papa pulls a carefully wrapped package from the side table. "For several months now," he begins, slowly sitting down again, "I've been working on a very special book of compositions."

"But, Papa, you're always working on music!" Wilhelm still hasn't finished his asparagus, but has his hands folded neatly on his lap like a little cherub.

"Ah, but this isn't any music. This is music for a special boy who has proven himself extremely skilled at the clavier in the past year. For a boy who has spent several hours every day in diligent practice and lessons, in addition to his studies at the Latin school. A boy who shows great promise."

Wilhelm looks as if he's about to burst with pride. He hiccups again, and everyone, even Tante Lena, laughs. Everyone except me.

Papa clears his throat. "And so, I would like to present this gift to a very gifted young boy, that he will grow to love music and serve God, give his life to music and God in the way that I have done."

Mama squeezes Papa's arm and brushes away a tear. Papa hands the package over to Wilhelm, who immediately begins tearing the paper to shreds.

"Wilhelm! You'll ruin the music!" Tante Lena warns. No one listens to her. Everyone is looking at the book that Wilhelm holds up for all to see. On the title page, in Papa's careful hand, is written

Little Clavier Book
for
Wilhelm Friedemann Bach
Begun in Cöthen
On January 22
Anno 1720

"Oh, Papa!" Wilhelm shouts, and flips through the pages of music written just for him. I have a lump in my throat. I can't speak, even if I wanted to. I stare at the cover of the book and try to imagine my name there along with Wilhelm's. I can't. It's too long—it would take up too much space and mess everything up.

"Papa, when can I begin?" Wilhelm clutches the book as if he'll never let it go.

It's as if the excitement over the book has erased all the deep creases in Papa's forehead—his worries about Prince Leopold and all the music he must write. Late into the night and early in the morning, always composing music or rehearsing it, his head so filled with music that I think there must be only the tiniest of spaces left for us. Like now, when he smiles at Wilhelm. "As soon as I tell the rest of the news." He leans over and points to the music. "See—I've begun with little preludes and dance settings, then moved on to a fugue and fantasias." He flips through the book. "And throughout are composition exercises, so that you can learn to compose as I do."

"What else, Johann?" Mama begins to gather the plates. Her mouth is pursed in concentration, as if she's expecting bad news.

"I have good news and bad," Papa begins. He and Mama exchange meaningful glances. I sometimes think they can read each other's mind.

"I'll begin with the good." He eyes Mama again. She stands as still as the statues of the bears above the door of the St. Agnus Church, only the bears don't hold armloads of plates. I try to picture them like that and almost start to laugh.

"The good news is that Prince Leopold has, as usual, invited the entire family to a special concert and party at the palace next Saturday evening, his birthday celebrations, of course. And I've composed a cantata just for the occasion, along with many other pieces. And the prince himself will play—"

"Hooray!" Wilhelm and Carl and Johann all shout and clap their hands.

Mama's mouth is still pursed. She's still like a statue with the plates. "And the bad?"

Papa looks down at his hands. The whole room is quiet; even Wilhelm's hiccups have stopped. "The prince is not feeling well. He's decided to take the waters at Carlsbad and has ordered myself and a small selection of the *capelle* to travel."

"When?" Mama's usually honey voice sounds pinched, as if someone's taken a cork and stopped the flow of it from the pot. Two years ago when Papa went to Carlsbad with the prince, she missed him terribly.

"In ten days." Papa's still looking down.

"How long?"

"The prince isn't sure. It depends on his health and the effect of the baths ... possibly until ... the beginning of July."

Mama drops a plate. Her face is pale. I'm sure she's never done anything so clumsy in her life. I am the one who drops the plates. She quickly bends down to pick up the pieces and I rush to help her.

"Mercy, Maria Barbara," says Tante Lena. "Calm yourself. It's only a little over a month. I'm sure you can bear life without a husband for that long. Heaven knows, I've certainly borne it longer."

74

Tante Lena is a spinster. No man would ever have her, and I suspect I will follow in her footsteps.

"Lena's right." Papa finally looks up and rises from his chair. The creases have returned; he looks so tired, as if he could sleep all day and the next and the next and still not have enough rest. "It isn't so long. Perhaps the prince will begin to feel the cure immediately!" He goes to Mama and touches her arm.

Mama just shakes her head and leaves the room. "Maria—" Papa goes after her and the younger boys begin to cry. Wilhelm grabs his book and goes to the clavichord and begins a trilling exercise.

"I'm not feeling so well myself." Tante Lena heads to her room.

I pick up the pieces and throw them in the bucket. Then I go to Carl and Johann, put my arms around them and hold them close. "Shh, shh ... it will be fine," I say. Will it? What's wrong with Mama? She was lonely the last time Papa was gone, but dropping plates and leaving the room? I take Johann on my knee and hold Carl close and think about all the things I didn't ask Papa. I didn't say one word during the entire meal, not that I ever do when Papa is there. I didn't tell him about the boys at the Latin school, or ask him about the music and the maze. I listen to Wilhelm's trills and stare at the fire. It's still crackling brightly. In fact, Johann's chubby cheeks are quite rosy with the heat. But when Mama rushed out I felt a chill, as if a sudden gust had blown in and put out the fire completely.

Five

Catharina

"WHAT IS IT THIS TIME?" I lean over the table to get a better look at the music Mama's copying, and my sewing drops to the floor.

She gives me a stern look, and I hurry to pick up Johann's little shirt. She answers by breaking into song, "'Heut ist gewiss ein guter Tag.'" She laughs. "It's from the birthday cantata for the prince."

"'Today Is a Good Day.'" I repeat the title and look out the window, at the blue sky and the fleecy clouds that remind me of Papa's white wigs. "It *is* a good day, isn't it?" The prince's birthday is in a few days. We're all in a grand, confused uproar because of it—music to copy, clothes to prepare. Lise is in quite a flap, rushing around the house muttering. And Mama seems to be back to normal. I know she'll miss Papa, but I can't help feeling a small twinge of happiness at the thought of a whole

77

month with her all to myself. I'll still have to share her with Tante Lena and the boys, but no Papa—maybe my heart will stop beating so hard during morning prayers. Seven days until he leaves.

"It will be a good day when I finally have this heap of music copied. Gracious—your papa's genius will be the death of my hand! A cantata with too many parts!" She places her quill pen beside the ink pot and flexes her long fingers.

"Mama ..." I draw my thread through the lace of Johann's shirt. It's one of my most tiresome chores—to remove the lace and sew all of it back on again after Lise has washed it. "Whatever became of the piece you were copying that day by the river?"

"Which one? There are so many—"

"The Concerto for Two Violins," I blurt out, and then look down and feel my face go hot.

"Oh, your papa said to leave that one until all of these birthday pieces are completed. I think he said it wouldn't be performed until after his return from Carlsbad." She looks at me curiously. "What's so special about it? You haven't even heard it!"

If only she knew about that time in morning prayers when I sang out, and the way I heard it, so clear but slightly out of tune, playing me out of the maze. If she could hear the way it runs through my head every blessed day! I can tell Mama many things, but not this. She'd think I was mad. I'm thinking so hard about all this that I completely miss the needle slipping from the satin into my skin.

"Oh, Catharina," she sighs, and rises to get a cloth and water. At least I kept the blood from staining Johann's shirt—that would have been a nice kettle of herring.

Mama kneels down and gently presses the cloth to my finger, looks at me with a strange expression, as if she's seeing me for the first time. "You need to play more with girls your age. There's Anna, Herr Rose's daughter. She's always at the concerts. Such a lovely girl—I'm sure she'd make a nice friend. Or maybe a nice young page will ask you to dance at the prince's noble ball." She gives me a wink.

I burst into laughter. I can't help myself. "I'd trip all over his poor feet and he'd never speak to me! Remember the dancing master?" Herr Kelterbrunnen was only trying to teach me how to execute the gavotte, but I somehow managed to trip and cause him to fall down on his rump on the floor.

"The poor Herr Kelterbrunnen! Such a fall!" Mama laughs, then straightens herself up and tries to look serious. "But really, you spend too much time with your old mama in the kitchen!"

"But, Mama! You're ever so young—"

"I'm thirty-six if I'm a day—"

"But you're ... you're my very *best* friend!"

Mama takes away the cloth—she's stopped the bleeding, of course—and returns to the music, shaking her head. "You ... set your heart too much on the things of this world, Catharina. The Scriptures say—"

"Oh, Mama, you're a person, not a thing! And I do have other friends, heaps of them, like, like ..."

She stops copying and looks up. I can think of no one. For once, I wish Tante Lena would wake from her nap and burst in on our talk. "Like ... like ... like the girl with the big nose!" I didn't mean for that to slip.

Mama bursts into laughter. That's what I love about her—she's like a fine day with fleecy clouds breezing in, just when you're expecting a storm. "Heavens, Catharina, you're one for a story!" She puts down her pen and settles into her chair. "Now, tell me all about this friend of yours."

"Well ... remember the penmanship assignment you gave me, the letter to a relative?"

"You didn't have it ready for the mail coach—"

"Because ... because ..." Suddenly I feel shy about telling her. Will she think I'm a dim-wit? "That day when I was walking Wilhelm to school—"

"You were angry when you came home."

"How did you know? I didn't say anything. You were busy baking."

She smiles. "I knew by the look on your face as soon as you walked in the door. I thought you would tell me about it. I was waiting."

"Oh, Mama. Wilhelm was wretched—he made me chase him through the marketplace with horse poop on my shoes." She smiles, and we both laugh a little. "I was so tired of brothers. And sometimes it seems so ... well, so ... unfair that I have to walk Wilhelm to school. I'd rather ..." I look up at her. How can I tell her? Will she tell Papa? "I'd rather attend the Latin school myself. I wonder if there's a place where girls attend the Latin school with the boys?" I try to ignore her shocked expression and just keep going before I lose my nerve. "I wish for a friend—"

"Just what I was saying. Herr Rose's daughter, Anna—"

"No, this girl isn't like Anna, who just smiles sweetly and looks pretty and hopes to catch a husband someday. This girl's different—she's not afraid to ... well, she's just not afraid." I swallow. "I made her up. I wrote a letter to her. It was kind of like writing a letter to myself, like a journal. It helped to make me feel better."

There's a quiet space before Mama speaks. "Girls in the Latin school with the boys! I would never have thought such a thing when I was your age. We just did as we were told. Where in heaven's name did you learn this, Catharina?"

I jab my needle into the thick satin, hard. I never should have said anything to Mama. "I don't know … the thought just came to me. After all, I've memorized practically all Wilhelm's Latin textbook—*abnuo, acuo, arguo* …"

Mama looks as if she's about to say something, then decides not to. She shakes her head. "Memorizing Latin! You'll never fail to surprise me." She sighs. "But things change, that's for certain." She sighs again, and looks as if she's thinking hard. "Maybe your friend does exist … somewhere."

I settle into the silence and carry on with my sewing, think about that girl living and breathing and maybe pricking her finger the way I did today. Did her mama stop the bleeding, just as mine did? Good old Mama. I knew she'd try to understand. But I won't tell her yet about the mirror in the gazebo, how for a moment I thought I saw the girl.

82

Or about the music that led us out, the notes of the Bach Double pulling me around corners and into the shadows, singing as I've never sung.

"Mama," I say quietly. There's one more thing I have to ask. "Will you go through the maze with me sometime?"

She nods, and smiles, and begins again to sing.

———

I tiptoe into Papa's music studio and take a deep breath. I've removed my heavy shoes, but this is no guarantee that I won't bump into a table and knock a red ink pot over a stack of manuscripts or send that line of raven quills and sharpening knife clattering to the floor. I move quickly to the huge desk where Papa writes most of his compositions. Of course, he tries them out later with instruments in the rehearsal chamber—that's what I heard that night I first heard the double concerto—but this is the private room where he sits and composes almost all his music and keeps some of his instruments. We children never enter. Even Mama seldom goes in, and Lise only when Papa requires a special cleaning.

I listen to the *capelle* playing up in the rehearsal chamber—that should take care of Papa for the next few hours. I should have waited until he was

83

safely away at the palace with all the extra rehearsals for the prince's birthday, but I couldn't wait until tomorrow. What do I hope to find? A glance at Papa's new violin, the one that may have played me out of the maze? No, he's probably playing it. The music for the double concerto? Maybe if I can see the second violin part that led me out of the maze—see it written out clearly in ink on a page— I'll find a clue or at least assurance that Papa actually composed it and that it doesn't just exist in my head. Maybe I *am* as mad as old Salome.

Everything is in order by Papa's desk: the stacks of blank paper, the ink pots with supplies of the ink powder he mixes with water, the raven quills and the knife I've seen him use to sharpen the quills and to erase mistakes after the ink has dried, the rulers and the small box of sand to blot the ink, the rastrum— the brass ruling pen he uses to make the staves on an empty page. I reach out and with a shaking hand stroke a raven quill. It trembles, too, as if it's still alive and could fly through the sky. But I mustn't stay too long here, although I could happily stand gazing at these beautiful things for an hour at least.

I tiptoe around the desk to the glass cupboard. This must be where he keeps the things he's still working on—here are the parts from the prince's birthday cantata. So the things still to be copied should be nearby—I fall to my knees by the nearest shelf to the cupboard and begin to thumb through a stack. Yes, these parts are incomplete, but they all seem to be in a very special order, probably by the required date of completion. But where, oh where, is the blessed Concerto for Two Violins? Surely it should be on the top of the stack—Mama began copying it only last week.

"What in heaven's name are you doing in here, girl?"

Papa stands in the doorway, his new violin tucked under his arm.

His face is very red. There is a deep crease between his eyebrows. He is so tall. I can't look at him anymore. I rise, keeping my eyes to the floor.

He says in a voice that is hushed but all the same roaring with rage, "I come to my studio to find some rehearsal copies, and what do I find but my own daughter down on her knees, snooping through my music like a thief! I demand an explanation! Fifteen men upstairs await my leadership, but I am willing to let them wait until I find out the meaning of this!"

"Johann, what is this all about?" It's Mama, standing behind him, her big eyes looming behind his perfect wig.

"Maria, I will ask you to kindly not interfere in the management of our unruly daughter, who must speak in explanation of this most despicable behaviour!"

If the highest judge in the highest court of Europe, if God Himself sitting on His throne in heaven asked these words, I would not be trembling more than I am now before Papa. My body is shaking all through. I think my knees will collapse, or I will faint, or worse, vomit red cabbage all over this shiny floor.

There is silence. And then a sound raises my gaze to the level of his new violin. It's Papa; in his annoyance with me, he's plucking his violin strings. I stare at the instrument, listen for each of the plucked sounds, clear and sure, travelling like friends over the cold space between my papa and me.

What is it about the music that helps me to raise my head and look him in the eye? Behind him Mama stands behind him, mouthing a word. *Truth.*

"If the truth be known, Papa—"

If the truth be known? Who is this speaking? Not Catharina Dorthea Bach, that's for certain.

The voice continues, "I very much wanted to have a look at the first movement of your Concerto for Two Violins in D Minor. I'm particularly interested in it. But I'm very sorry for trespassing in your private studio."

Probably the most I've ever said to Papa in my entire life.

Now he looks as if he will faint from the shock of my speech. "Well, I had no idea you had such interest in my musical works, nor the tongue to speak of it. For your information, that concerto is now in the hands of Herr Colm in the palace library. He's to complete a set of fair copies for the first performance of that piece after our return from Carlsbad. You simply could have asked this question of me, rather than snooping through my room. I ask you never to enter my studio unaccompanied again. Now, if you will excuse me, I must attend to my rehearsal. Maria, please attend to your daughter." He takes a stack of music and clatters down the long hallway.

I take step after wooden step toward Mama and collapse into her arms.

Hannah

Finally. The noon bell. I rush past Melissa and Tracy and company giggling and hanging around Jeremy and Ben at the back of the classroom.

"Look at Hannah," says Jeremy, "rushing off to practise on the squawk box."

"She doesn't have *time* to just hang out talking," says Melissa. "She has to practise for an important concert, or maybe study for a test." They collapse into giggles.

I want to ignore them and breeze out the door as cool as Bridget the Perfect or Hilary the Head Girl, but I can't help turning back. "At least I have better things to do with my time than to stand around insulting people!" Out in the hallway I hear words like "weird" and more giggling and "I'm *so* crushed!" Why didn't I just keep quiet? Now they'll probably hate me even more. But all I want to do right now is get to the library. I've tried every day since last Tuesday, but it's been locked. Maybe Mrs. Friesen forgot again today.

I glance into the office on my way. Ms. Lockport sees me and gives me a winning smile. She has very white teeth and is wearing pale pink lipstick to match her pale pink outfit. She beckons me into the office.

"Hi, Hannah. I'm so glad you happened by," she says. "Remember that little proposal I mentioned to you on the way to your lesson on Monday, about playing in the assembly?"

I nod and gulp and glance at the calendar. It's already Friday. Marie's fiddle party is in one week, and Dad's still holding off giving me permission to go. How will I face Marie on the bus on Monday with no answer? I can just picture myself marching up to her. "Sorry, Marie, I'd love to come but my dad's afraid your family might kidnap me." Or something equally lame.

"I was just wondering if you checked with your teacher and your father about playing yet?" Ms. Lockport's earrings match her suit and her lipstick.

"Not really." I shake my head. "Sorry. I will at my lesson this Monday, but there's always so much music to cover in my lesson and my teacher says—"

"Such a wonderful opportunity for you to share your music with the other kids. I was so excited that I mentioned my idea to Mr. Griggs and he thought it was wonderful, too, and we got out the schedule, and wouldn't you know it, there's a little blank on the last Tuesday in March, just waiting for you to fill it!"

She looks as if she's just handed me a cake and balloons. How can I pop them? "That's really nice of you, Ms. Lockport. But I'll have to ask my dad—"

"I should think a girl your age would be able to make some decisions on her own." She drums her fingernails on the counter. Pale pink, to match everything else.

I push up my glasses and stare at the calendar. One month.

"Hannah, I'll tell you what. I'll give your dad a little call this very afternoon and see what he says. I can't imagine he'll have a problem with it. What parent wouldn't want his child to perform for the whole school? If he says yes, can I count you in?"

She looks so hopeful. And if I say no, she might not be so nice about giving me rides to my lessons every week. I push up my glasses and nod. I just want to get out of here before she signs me up for volleyball and the science club.

"I'll give your dad a call right after lunch." She beams as I make my escape.

I have to get to the library. The way things are going today, I know it will be closed, but I have to try. How do I get roped into these things? In one month, I'm going to play my violin for the whole school. What will I play? Mom always told her students, "When you're performing in nerve-racking situations, play a review piece. Everyone always loves 'Humoresque.'" "Humoresque" would be perfect, even though I hadn't even learned it yet when she said that. It sounds hard but it's pretty

90

easy, hardly any shifts even, except on the second page. Who will I get to play piano? I think about Melissa's braces and my stomach starts to twist. Maybe Dad will say no.

All the library blinds are closed and it looks locked. My heart sinks, but I try the door anyway and walk right in.

To piano music. A Polish dance—I remember Mom's friend Michael playing it. Mr. Franckowiak is hunched right over, in his own world. I sneak behind the computers and some shelves, straight to my spot by the heating vent. The book about Hilary the Head Girl is still there, too. I take it in my hands and close my eyes and listen to the music. He ends the piece with just as much oomph as Michael always did. By the time he finished we were always dancing around the room.

Without stopping he launches right into another piece—"The Girl with the Flaxen Hair" by Debussy—we have it on a CD, and there's an arrangement for violin that Mom taught her older students. And even though the library piano is really out of tune and it's so cold outside, the music reminds me of those shimmery summer days when we packed up the picnic basket and Mom drove us out to Uncle Ted and Aunt Beth's place near

Kitchener, to the Corn Maze, because Mom always loved to walk through it.

And after we'd laughed and stumbled our way through, Mom always making it through first, I'd lie on our blanket by the maze, and sometimes I thought I could hear the corn grow. Time moved so slowly. You could scoop it up in your hand and it wouldn't wriggle away. I remember once looking over at Mom and Dad on the other side of the blanket, napping with their arms around each other. I squeezed a handful of grass in my fist. I wanted to keep everything just the way it was. But then the time always came to leave, and I'd stand up, let the grass fall from between my fingers as we folded up the blanket and packed it into the car. We'd drive back to Toronto, and then fall always came, and winter, and the spring that Mom—

"You can come out from hiding." Mr. Franckowiak has stopped playing. "I'm not so very frightening."

Slowly, I put the book back on the shelf and walk over to the piano. "I'm … I'm sorry. I didn't mean to interrupt your playing. How did you know I was in here?"

"Oh, you didn't interrupt. At the conservatory, in Kraków, I played for audiences all the time …" He's so small, but it's as if his almost black eyes are looking past this puny town, up and over the grain elevators, over the fields to an ocean far away.

"Where's Kraków?"

"In Poland. Where I came from, many years ago." He slumps a little, as if he's just lost something and given up hope of ever finding it. "You've heard of it?"

"I knew a girl once who took Polish dancing."

He nods. "You didn't ever try our dances?"

I can feel myself blushing. "I'm not very good at dancing." I stare down at the yellowing piano keys, then up at his face. He looks so disappointed. "But ... I can play the violin, sort of, and there are some dances my mom used to play ... by Bartók. Were they from your country?" I hum a bit, the last section that's like a hopping whirlwind. I remember Mom's long fingers just flying over the fingerboard, her bow hopping on the strings as she played the spicatto notes. I keep humming, and he turns back to the piano and comes right in at the place that I'm humming. We sing and play all the way to the last note, where I'd always get goosebumps when Mom's bow lifted off the string.

Mr. Franckowiak turns around and grins. "Bartók's 'Roumanian Dances.' Not too far away from my home." He flexes his fingers. "Anyone who can sing like that must know how to dance." He smiles. "You … must be the violinist from the bus. Marie told me about you—"

"Ms. Dumont! How do you know her?"

"Oh, we met up once at the bowling alley when she was coming off a shift and my wife and I were treating ourselves to butter tarts after a game. Somehow we got talking about music. You should see her family fiddle. In fact, they're having a birthday party in a week."

"I know! I'm … invited." If Dad knows that Mr. Franckowiak, who plays Bartók and Bach and Debussy just as well as anyone I've ever heard, is going to be there, maybe …

"Are you going?"

He's stood up and is gathering his music books. "Wouldn't miss it." He reaches for his pile of keys and drops them, then picks them up and heads for the door. "The first bell will be going off soon. You be careful about leaving here, Miss …"

"Hannah."

"The principal's given me special permission to come in here noon hours because I have no piano at home, but you … that's a different story. No kids allowed in here lunch hours. I could get in trouble, too. Be careful when you leave." He smiles and winks. "Now, from Bartók to the boys' washroom. Goodbye, Hannah. Hope to see you next Saturday."

"Bye, Mr. Franckowiak."

He winks again, his hand on the knob, and then he's gone. I need to make a smooth exit, too—Mrs. Friesen will be coming in here, and I can't be late for my class or everyone will stare. I slip out the door. My stomach goes loose with relief when I see the hallway empty, then tightens again when I see one straggler rush in from outside. It's Melissa, her cheeks pink against her smart blue coat and scarf. I quickly close the library door, but it's too late—I can see her braces gleam down the hallway as she gives me a smile that tells me she won't keep this secret for long.

I polish my violin for the party, thinking about how excited Marie was when I told her I could go. "It'll start early in the afternoon on Saturday and go all night!" she said. "Make sure you get there in time for Aunt Bernadette's famous *tourtière*!"

"Meat pie—yum!" I said, glad at last for all my years in French immersion.

I wipe away the fingerprints and the rosin. The smell of the polish reminds me of Mom. I imagine that my violin is very old and has passed through the hands of many people over hundreds of years, since about seventeen hundred and something. I imagine the wood all shiny under candlelight, like the violin that reminded me of Mom's at the girl's ball. I run my cloth over the shoulders and down the neck—what other hands have touched it before me? But then I remember that snotty-nosed kid from the back of the third violin section in the Junior Orchestra who owned it before me and he got it new. Dumb old three-quarter size. I give it one last wipe and shut it away in its case.

Mom's violin, on the other hand ... I tiptoe out into the hallway and lean over the banister, imagine it sitting behind the closed door of Dad's room. Dad's fixing the hinge on the bathroom door downstairs; I can hear the sound of the drill. He's been in a pretty good mood ever since he got the call last Friday from Ms. Lockport about the assembly. He fixed his extra-special spaghetti sauce, and I helped with the carrot sticks and the apple crisp. I was sprinkling crumbs on the apple crisp when he said, "So I hear you're going to give a performance?"

I stopped sprinkling. "Do I have to?"

"You used to like playing for other people." He gave the sauce a hard stir.

"For Mom's other students and kids from group class. Not a whole assembly of kids who don't know anything about me and make fun all the time."

He sighed. "What are they saying?"

"I don't know ... it's as if they've never seen a real violin before."

"Well, they probably haven't. This would be a great chance—"

"Oh, I know. Ms. Lockport says the same thing. But it'll just be really nerve-racking." I think of Melissa's smile that day in the hall. She hasn't said anything yet about me sneaking out of the library, but I'm sure she's up to something. She keeps looking over at me and smirking. "I was hoping you'd say no—"

Dad laughed. "Play something easy. When you're performing in nerve-racking situations, play a review piece. Everyone always loves—"

"'Humoresque.' I know, I know. That's what Mom—" I stopped quickly. Dad looked away as soon as I said her name. He probably didn't even realize he was quoting her when he first said it.

"Who'll you get to play the piano?"

"Actually," I said, chopping up the carrots any which way. They never turn out the same, no matter how hard I try. "Collector's Carrot Sticks," Mom used to call them. "No two are ever alike." She'd be in with Dad on this assembly thing. She'd think I should play. And it's true, I used to like to play for people—when did things change? "Actually … the custodian at our school is really good."

"Really?" Dad looked skeptical. "You mean he plays 'O Canada' at assemblies."

"No! You should hear him. He went to the conservatory in Kraków, and I've heard him play Debussy and Bach and even Bartók's 'Roumanian Dances' just like Michael, and he's going to Marie's party—"

"He went to the Kraków Conservatory?" Dad looked doubtful but just a little impressed.

I convinced Dad to get on the phone the next day with Mr. Franckowiak. Either Bach or Mr. Franckowiak won him over. Now it's all arranged for me to go to the party—Mr. Franckowiak and his wife are going to give me a ride—even though Dad still wouldn't agree to come himself, insisting that the bathroom door was crying out to be finished.

I listen to the drill, lean over the banister, and look over at Dad's room, door shut tightly as usual.

I hesitate for a moment. Then I'm inside and looking at Dad's jeans and T-shirts and sweatshirts piled around on the floor. Where would he keep her violin? I check in the usual places—under the bed and in the closet. Of course, nothing there.

A few short silences break up Dad's drilling. Where would he keep it? I look at my reflection in the round mirror, as if the girl in there will have an answer. I hum the Bach Double, as if that will somehow crack the mirror and reveal a secret door. Right. I put my palms on the dresser and lean forward to look at the new zit that's popping out on my forehead. Another silence in the drilling—I'm just about to give up when I hear the bats.

When we first moved here, the faint rustling in the walls freaked me out. After a while I pretended that instead of scary dark things hanging upside down, the rustling in the walls was the sound of ladies from a long time ago in silk dresses having tea. I put my ear against the wall, and even though the drilling starts up again I can hear them in there—*scritch, scritch.* I look up. Right above me is a cupboard with a door made of wooden slats. It creaks when I tug it open—some shelves with Dad's camera and some photo albums—probably the ones with pictures of Mom. I'm about to close it again when I notice a space under the bottom shelf.

I have her case open on the bed in a snap. The picture of the three of us licking triple-scoop Rocky

Road ice cream at the Beaches is still in its usual place behind one of her bows. I quickly undo the Velcro strap and ease her violin from its blue satin drawstring bag.

Drill, drill. Dad will be coming up here to read pretty soon. Mom told me it was made in 1720 in Germany—the maker's name was Aman, I think. I forget his first name. I run my finger over the thin line between the scroll and the neck. Mom explained to me once that it's the cut they made to change it from a baroque-period violin, the kind that had a different neck, to a modern violin. I pluck a few of the strings like a guitar. Then I put it under my chin and I can smell that lotion she used to wear, just a faint whiff of vanilla. I close my eyes and the Bach Double crashes through my head— tinny and jarring, not anything like real sound. I feel dizzy. I close my eyes and think I see the girl from the ball again, the one I heard singing, only now she's in a room looking scared. I think I'm going to faint. Mom's violin might fall, it's going to slip and fall on the floor and splinter—

The drilling has stopped. The walls and lamp and green curtains and Dad's University of Toronto sweatshirt on the bed spin around me, but somehow I manage to grab the drawstring bag and with one hand make it hang open so I can get the violin back inside. A small envelope slides to the floor. I scoop it up and am about to cram it into my pocket—what could be inside?—when I realize that Dad might miss it. Dad—he could already be at the bottom of the stairs. The more I try to rush, the slower I move. I force my hands to jam the envelope and the violin back into the bag and the bag back in the case, to fasten the Velcro strap, to shut and zip the case and get it all back into its hiding place. Then I'm back in my room with the door shut, panting, my nose pressed against the cold window in the dark. My heart is rushing fast to the beat of Mom playing the Bach Double. I try to ignore her, look out at the stars, at the blinking one, as Dad's firm footsteps make their way, so slowly, up the stairs.

Six

Hannah

DAD PUSHES UP HIS GLASSES, a sure sign of nervousness. "You'll bring her home before too late?" He looks down at Mr. Franckowiak and at his even shorter wife.

Mr. Franckowiak pulls his pom-pom toque over his big ears and smiles up at Dad. With his parka hood up and his scarf wrapped around and his toque so low, only his dark eyes and bushy eyebrows show. He keeps blinking—I think he's nervous, too. I wish Dad could hear him play. "I forgot to tell you on the phone that we turn into pumpkins at ten o'clock, although these parties usually go until the wee hours—"

"But it's starting in the afternoon. What on earth do they do all that time?"

Mr. Franckowiak laughs. "You'll have to come along sometime and see. Now, speaking of starting early"—he looks at his watch—"we really must be going if we want to get a piece of Aunt Bernadette's *tourtière*. A pleasure to meet you, Dr. Waters." He nods to Dad and turns to the door. I breathe a sigh of relief. I keep thinking Dad's going to change his mind at the last minute, but now it looks as if we're really leaving. Mr. F. seems to be good at making quick exits.

"Don't worry, we'll have her home safe and sound." Mrs. Franckowiak beams at Dad. When she smiles, her whole face crinkles up. Once we're safe inside the very old but spotless car, I turn back and see Dad standing at the window. I wave and he waves back. I turn forward as we move out of the driveway, then quickly turn around to see him sitting at the kitchen table with his head in his hands.

I quickly face forward. I have an ache at the back of my throat. I swallow a few times but it doesn't help. I hug my violin case close.

"How long have you played the violin?" asks Mrs. Franckowiak, looking back so that she can see me.

"My mom taught me when I was four," I say automatically, and then wish I hadn't said anything about Mom. Now I'll have to explain.

"Now you study in the city, yes?" Mr. Franckowiak smiles at me in the mirror. Maybe Dad or Marie already told them about Mom. Anyway, I'm grateful to them for not going into it.

I nod.

"Have you studied those 'Roumanian Dances'? You sure sang them as if you know them. I don't think that old school library's ever heard the likes of that!"

I shake my head. "No. Mom played them ..." Why can't I keep my mouth shut about her?

"What are you studying now?"

"The Bach Double. I can play it all the way through on my own from memory, but whenever I have to play for Mr. Dekker I get all nervous and flub it up."

"It's a very special piece. When I was a student at the conservatory I heard many performances of it," says Mr. F.

"Did you ever hear anyone make a mistake?"

"Oh, sure—even the greatest artists make mistakes when they're performing. The trick is to keep going as if nothing happened." We rumble over a bridge, and I think about what it would be like to actually play for people and not worry about making a mistake. "Beautiful country, isn't it? Reminds me of Poland in some ways."

I look out the window. The river's partially frozen, with icicles like flowers hanging from the reeds. "I've never seen this before. My dad doesn't drive, so we don't get out much, except places we can walk—"

"Well then, you and your father will just have to come along with us sometime on our Sunday drive." Mrs. Franckowiak pats my hand. Her hand on mine feels warm, moist, nice. We drive up the hill from the river, and all around a big whiteness opens up—fields with grass poking through, and the sun making it all sparkle so I have to shield my eyes. *Make this piece sparkle.* Mom said that to me about "Two Grenadiers," to her students about "Humoresque."

I lean forward and a question bursts out. "I have to play 'Humoresque' for this assembly at school on the last Tuesday in March. Could you play the piano?"

"Of course." He smiles, nodding in the rearview mirror, his pom-pom bobbing up and down. "Everyone always loves 'Humoresque.'"

⌐━⌐

"Find a partner for the 'Red River Jig'!" shouts a man I think might be Marie's uncle Maurice. As soon as we stepped in the door a few hours ago, my glasses fogged up, right when Marie was trying to introduce me to everyone. How embarrassing. I had to take them off to wipe them with a ratty tissue from my pocket, and everyone was a blur. Even though I have my glasses back on, I've been in a blur of music and dancing and food ever since.

Mr. and Mrs. Franckowiak are getting up to dance as if they've done this all their lives. And the fiddlers in the corner—Grandpa Joe, Marie, and another uncle—are tuning up and fooling around playing. I take another bite of Saskatoon pie. I've never tasted anything like it—I can taste summer in it, and something like deep ravines and wildness that I can't explain. The table in the kitchen's piled up with as much Saskatoon pie as anyone could eat, and *boulette,* which is a meatball soup, and Aunt Bernadette's *tourtière* and Uncle Fred's *baigne,* a kind of fried bread, and Metis soup that's more like a stew because it's so thick with hamburger and carrots and celery. "Just pile up your plate as high as you want," said Aunt Bernadette with a big grin, wiping her hands on her spotless apron. When I asked, "How do you keep it so spotless when you have to make all that food?" she just shrugged and gave me a mysterious smile. I followed her advice about piling up my plate. I didn't think I'd ever get another chance to eat so well again, thinking of Dad's spaghetti sauce.

I scrape the last of the deep purple berries from my plate. "Do you want to dance?" asks Billy, who's about four years younger than me. I shake my head. I can't believe his bravery. I tried the "Duck Dance" with him soon after we got here. Marie showed me the basic one-two-three step. It seemed pretty easy and I could get it slowly, but as soon as the fiddles started up and everything got faster, my feet got all tangled up, and when I tried to duck to get under Billy's arm, I knocked over a can of pop. Luckily, it was empty.

"Tease the cats with us," says Billy. I shake my head, and after a moment he just shrugs and runs out of the room with a bunch of younger cousins following as if he's the Pied Piper.

I look at the tip of my violin case sticking out from behind the door of the room where all the coats are piled on the bed. Marie hasn't said anything about teaching me yet. She's too busy playing the fiddle with Grandpa Dumont. She keeps looking over at him and smiling. He has his eyes closed, but even if they were open it wouldn't matter because Marie says he's almost blind. You'd never know that he turned ninety-two today, though. He was dancing like anything to "Drops of Brandy," and now his fingers are flying as fast as the feet kicking up all around me. I try to finger the notes of the tune on my jeans with my left hand. It's as fast as the first movement of the Bach Double. Faster.

I make sure no one is watching and slip into the room with the coats and my violin. I close the door, then take my violin out and hold it like a guitar and try to finger along—at least get a few notes. Then I put it under my chin and bow really lightly over the strings so that no one will hear. But it all rushes by me like the scenery outside a train window. If I had notes in front of me, I'd be able to get it. Mom said I was a pretty good sight reader, and I think the notes are all just in easy first position. But it's like listening to the women jabbering in Italian in the store near our place in Toronto. I can't pick anything out. How could I have been so stupid to think I could even bring my violin and play along with the others? They probably took one look at my violin and laughed.

I'm about to shove it in my case again when Marie peeks around the door. "I thought you might be hiding in here," she says. "Come on, I want to show you something."

"I … I can't," I say, nodding to where the music's coming from. "It's too fast." She's probably sorry she asked me in the first place. I squeeze the handle of my violin case, as if it can somehow transport me out of here to the safety of my room.

She just laughs. "Don't be silly." She's holding her fiddle with one hand and takes my hand with the other and pulls me out of the room, through the kitchen, and up the dark stairway to her room. "Time for you to learn 'St. Anne's Reel,'" she says, sitting on the bed and putting her fiddle up to her chin.

"But you're missing the dancing! And Grandpa's party and playing tunes with him! And what about the cake? Billy said there were ninety-two candles—"

"Don't worry," she says, smiling. "There's no rush—it'll go all night—"

"But Mr. and Mrs. Franckowiak turn into pump kins at ten, and my dad—"

"Uncle Charlie used to say there's no sense worrying about the pigs getting loose until they're actually squealing in the yard. Did you see Jack and Elena dancing? We've got at least another couple of hours. Now, listen carefully." She plays a little blip of music, just the beginning of the tune they were jigging to. I play back a few notes, as if I'm answering a question she's just asked. Not quite right, though. She plays it again, and this time I finger along as she plays, and then when it's my turn I get it right.

"You've done this before." She smiles and adds another bit.

I answer back, right on the first try this time. All those years—"Go Tell Aunt Rhody," "Song of the Wind," "Lightly Row," "May Song," Mom giving me the phrase and me answering back—it was exactly like this, like picking out shiny bits of smooth glass from the sand. All those notes she gave me, like presents. What happened to them? Where did they go when she …

I have to concentrate on getting the next part of the tune. Each time it's longer, adding to what I've already got. After I get the whole first part, we play it around a few times before Marie starts giving me the second section. I close my eyes and take each section of music. Sometimes I flub up and she has to give it to me again. We just go deeper and deeper—she gives and I take. And then, way deep down somewhere, I know I've got the whole thing. We play it around again and again—I lose track of how many times. It's that old familiar Ferris wheel feeling—each time around I know where I'm going to end up, even though some of the dips and swoops are a little scary. "Go Tell Aunt Rhody,"

"May Song," the gleam of Mom's violin when I opened my eyes after learning a new piece. Mom …

I open my eyes. Not Mom but Marie, grinning like a jack-o'-lantern or one of those Ches-something cats. "That's a record for learning 'St. Anne's' if I ever saw it," she says. "Come on, let's go downstairs. I want Grandpa to hear you and you can play for another round of the 'Red River Jig'—"

"I'll forget. I'll screw up."

Marie laughs. Her laughs are like rests in music, giving you a chance to catch your breath. "Who cares? You think Grandpa Joe never makes a mistake? It's the beat that counts, that drives people to get up off their chairs and kick up their feet. C'mon."

There's a break in the dancing—people are in the kitchen helping themselves to more pie. Marie marches me right up to where he's sitting. "Grandpa Joe, this is my friend Hannah Waters. She just learned 'St. Anne's' and she's going to play it for the next set."

My heart's pumping somewhere up in my nose. Good thing it's big enough to hold all that extra blood. "Happy Birthday," I say, and reach out my hand. Is a handshake the right thing for the grandson of Gabriel Dumont? Probably not. I should curtsy instead. Or bow, as one would to a prince.

Up close, I can see how old he really is. "Waters, eh?" He lifts his gnarled hand and touches my arm. I jump.

Marie laughs, "Grandpa!" She moves to place his hand in mine, into a regular handshake, but he leaves it firmly on my arm. I wonder if he can feel how keyed up it is. "Like a cat, ready to spring," Mom would say. "You have to learn to relax, to let it go."

"Waters." His eyes are open, but I sense that he's looking past me, outside to the fields. "Frozen muscle, frozen river. Then the fiddler plays and the ice melts, there's a warm wind, the river begins to flow. Moving waters. People dance." He slowly lifts his hand from my arm and takes his own fiddle and bow. He smiles and nods for me to join in. He starts in on "St. Anne's Reel" and his arm *is* like a melting river, moving so fast between the strings.

"Go ahead." Marie laughs and lifts her violin to her chin.

People drift in from the kitchen and start to dance. I concentrate on their feet moving, on keeping my beat going in time to their kicking feet. I look over at Marie and laugh. I lose track of how many notes I miss. No one cares. They're all having too much fun dancing. I forget how many times we play "St. Anne's Reel," around and around. I watch those kicking feet. Once I glance up to the faces and see Mr. Franckowiak smiling and winking at me, as if our ten o'clock deadline has just melted into the river.

Catharina

"Catharina, will you please tell the boys to stop making such a ruckus and straighten up their clothes? The carriage for the palace will be here any minute." Mama looks up from the cantata part she's copying. Papa made a change at yesterday's rehearsal, and Mama and Herr Colm have been copying the correction ever since. Papa is already at the palace, warming up the *capelle* for the grand birthday concert.

"Yes, Mama." I break away from the mirror, where I've been trying to make my wig and my satin overdress look half presentable. If only I could look a little like Mama—so distinguished, with the wreath of carnations around her wig and the blue gown that matches her eyes. I glance back in the mirror. If only I weren't so … plain.

"In my day, girls did their mothers' bidding immediately, without pausing to hanker after themselves in the mirror first," remarks Tante Lena from her chair by the door. She's been sitting and waiting for the carriage for an hour at least, all ready in her best dull green gown, not helping anyone. I wish I had a sharp reply but am tongue-tied as usual and march off to round up the boys.

Wilhelm is playing the clavichord. Carl and Johann are running in circles around it, speeding up when he speeds ups, slowing when he slows. Wilhelm plays faster and faster and soon they're in a complete frenzy—I can just see Johann falling any minute now and ripping the lace I so carefully sewed on.

"Mama says to stop!" I say in my loudest, firmest voice, which is barely above a whisper. I could be speaking to the wind, for all the attention they give me. I clear my throat and try again. "Wilhelm! Johann! Carl! The prince's birthday concert! The carriage—"

They run in circles and giggle, and a scream wells up in my throat. I realize suddenly that to my brothers I'm mostly invisible, except, of course, when I trip over my skirts to make them laugh. I stamp my foot hard on the floor. I walk over to grab them by their little chubby arms and give them a good shake …

Wilhelm stops playing and looks up. Johann and Carl are quiet. Could they actually be paying attention to me? But no, they're looking up and behind me. I turn around to see Mama in the doorway. She hasn't said a word but wears a slight frown.

"I'm sorry, Mama," Wilhelm sputters and stands up from the clavichord and straightens his coat. The younger boys run to Mama and wrap their arms about her skirts. "We're sorry."

"Yes, yes, never mind." She removes them gently from her skirts. "You should have listened to your sister in the first place." They glance over at me and Wilhelm sticks out his tongue. "Come along." Mama bustles them ahead of her. She missed seeing Wilhelm's tongue. "We musn't be late for the concert—after all the work your poor papa has put into it, weeks of composing, all the new music. The carriage is waiting."

I follow along behind and lift my skirts so they don't trail in the dust on the steps leading down to the landing. All my excitement about the birthday is fading into the dull green of Tante Lena's dress. It's always the same—concert, feasting, dancing. Plunk, plunk, plunk, down the stairs with my load of skirts.

"Mama says to stop playing and come *immediately*," the girl would say in quite a calm voice, calm but firm, which would cause them to obey straightaway.

"*Immediately*. Now there's a good word," I say, stepping into the carriage.

"Next time," she says from my reflection in the carriage window, winking as the carriage pulls us away to the ball.

⸻

"Today is a good day ..." sings Madame Monjou, the soprano from Berlin. Her voice is just as huge as she is—I listen to it slide up to the high ceiling in the great Hall of Mirrors. I pretend her voice is mine; if I open my mouth to speak to my brothers, out will come not the sorry whisper I used to scold them earlier, but this singing voice—huge and able to fill up a great hall. Wilhelm would tell all the boys at the Latin school, and they'd say, "Here comes the girl with the glorious voice. Such a voice!" Word would spread, and people would come from distant towns to hear me.

I look in the mirror framed by swirling leaves of dark wood and see the reflection of the prince up in his balcony, with his long wig and his special velvet robe, smiling with his cheeks flushed. He's twenty-six years old today. Papa will be glad that he's enjoying the music. I can see Papa in the mirror, too. His lips are pursed in concentration as he plays the violin and leads the *capelle,* but I can tell that he's happy with the concert, the way he's moving with the music and even looking up from his music and smiling over at Herr Spiess.

I give the girl in the mirror a little nod and say inside my head, "Hello. Can you catch Madame Monjou's voice and give it to me? It's sliding right by you."

"No, of course not. She's trilling too fast. Have you ever tried a trill?"

I shake my head a little. "I've wished ..."

"Sometime when Mama is at the market and Tante Lena is sleeping, go into the back pantry and try a trill or two. Only the garlic will hear."

I almost burst into a not-inside-my-head giggle at the thought of garlic ears but catch Tante Lena frowning at me in the mirror. I look ahead and concentrate on Herr Fischer, the bass, who now sings together with Madame Monjou in a duct. The two voices wind around each other like ... like ...

I look up to the ceiling and can barely see her in the mirror, looking down on me as if she's a star. "What does this music remind you of?" I ask.

"Two violins. The Concerto for Two Violins, of course, which has trills, which you've sung in your head a hundred times, ever since you heard Papa compose it. What if, after the concert, you asked Madame Monjou to teach you a trill?"

I almost laugh out loud again at the thought of me speaking to the beautiful singer, who stands so tall in her emerald green gown, sending her voice over this crowd of strangers. The hall is suddenly drowned in applause. Oh, how the people clap! For her beautiful voice, and for my own papa's music. Mama's cheeks are flushed—it looks as if she'll never be finished with clapping. Papa and Herr Spiess and the rest have to bow several times. Then Papa gestures up to the prince, where he sits clapping with his mother, Her Highness Princess Gisela Agnes. The prince is so handsome, with his long curls. He stands and takes the most graceful bow, and everyone claps louder. I imagine that he is bowing to me, asking, "Dearest Catharina, would you do me the honour of dancing this gavotte?"

"Why, of course, dear Prince, I would be most honoured." In my mind I curtsy most gracefully, and take his hand and—

"Catharina, everyone's leaving to see the marzipan figurine. Everyone except you!" Wilhelm pokes my shoulder and runs away. I stand up and see that he's right; everyone is filing away for the grand feast and the noble ball. I wonder how big the court pastry maker has made the figurine of the prince this year. My stomach rumbles when I think of the almond pastry, so high! Every year, as the prince's age increases, so does the marzipan model of him. And there's chocolate torte and fruit torte and figs and pears, too, and oranges especially picked from the Orangery by Herr Felici.

I glance up once more to the ceiling, to say goodbye. It's the way I always end my mirror game at Papa's concerts.

"What do you see up there?" I recognize the emerald gown in the mirror before her speaking voice. Madame Monjou! I look desperately for Mama to rescue me, but she's already left for the feast; only a few servants are left cleaning the hall.

"I ... I ..." I look down and study the way one blond strip of wood overlaps another. Speak! But how can I tell her of my mirror game? How silly it is—something a child would play. I want to run, but my reflection holds me in place with a thumping heart, my tongue frozen.

"I remember such a mirror ceiling in my very first public concert," she says. "I was so frightened before all those people. I was afraid I'd open my mouth and nothing would come out. Then I pretended that they were invisible and I was singing only to myself up on the ceiling. And I was able to lift up my head, face those people, and sing." She sends a trill up to the mirror and laughs. "Now they pay me money to have such fun." She sings another few notes and laughs again. "Try it."

I open my mouth and there's my voice—thin as a charred pastry without the filling in it. I hang my head.

"Pretend that you're a well, and your voice is coming from a place deep inside you—somewhere at the bottom of your feet!" She sings the beginning of "Today …"

How many times have I heard Mama hum this as she copies? How many times did I hear Papa play this as he composed it? I sing the first phrase, just as far as Madame Monjou has done.

"Fine!" she says. "There was something about the way you looked at me during the concert that told me about your voice." She sings the next phrase. I sing it back to her, then go even further along than what she's given me, catch myself, and feel my face go hot.

"Now try with me from the beginning." She touches my shoulder, her hand heavy with rings.

"You can't slouch so. Your body is your instrument—have you ever heard of a sagging violin? Now, stand tall—yes, that's better."

We sing it all the way through, stopping in one section to work on the notes and practise the trills. I sing to the girl up in the ceiling—I feel so tall that I could be even higher than the ceiling, Madame Monjou's voice and mine floating up on some cloud, or higher, up to the stars and beyond.

"Bravo!" she shouts, after the last note has died in the hall. "I haven't even asked your name. Forgive me."

"Catharina," I say so easily. I'm still up on the ceiling somewhere. I glance at myself in the wall mirror. Do I look a little taller?

"I must introduce you to the composer of this work. Have you ever met the great Johann Sebastian Bach?"

Now I'm back to studying the floor.

"Come," she continues, leading me by the arm to the banquet room. "You must meet him. At this rate, you'll be ready for a professional position in a few years, and his influence could be enormously helpful in placing you."

I'm crashing to the ground with each step closer to Papa. "Excuse me, Madame Monjou," I say, wondering where my stammer has gone. "I must tell you ... he ... Johann Sebastian Bach, I mean ... is ... my ... papa."

She stops in front of the marzipan sculpture of the prince. "I should have known—of course you would be his daughter. Well, then he knows all about your talent and will no doubt find you a position someday—"

"No! I can't even speak to him. It's hard for me to explain ..." What if I turn mute before Madame Monjou? But she waits so patiently for me to speak, although I'm sure there are crowds of admirers waiting for her in the other room. I clear my throat. "Have you ever ... wanted ... with all your might to speak, and opened your ... your mouth, and ... and ... nothing ... comes out but a few sputters?"

She's quiet for a while and then nods. "I understand," she says, and I think about her first concert, her fear of opening her mouth and nothing coming out. "You need to tell him what it is you want to do most in the world, about the deep well of voice in you that must come out. Only you can tell him. Promise me that someday ... when you're ready ... you'll tell him."

I nod. She touches my shoulder blade, so lightly. "Tall," she whispers and smiles, and then turns away and slips into the crowd just as a red-faced page approaches. He stops in front of the figurine of Prince Leopold. It is magnificent—almost the size of six-year-old Carl—with miniature marzipan curls and a marzipan robe.

"Too bad the poor prince will be chopped to pieces and eaten before the night is through," he says with a laugh.

I can't help laughing too. "And on his twenty-sixth birthday! Such a shame!" I answer the page without even thinking.

He looks at me and laughs again. "I was wondering ..." he says very slowly, "if you would do me the honour of dancing this gavotte?"

Heavens! The dancing master said I was hopeless as a toad at the gavotte. "Some feet aren't meant to execute the dance," he said, shaking his head and looking down at my oversize feet. This was after the tripping and falling on rump incident. And now, here I am at the noble ball, receiving my first invitation. I begin to shake my head, then remember the sound of my voice in the great hall, and Madame Monjou, the feel of her rings against my shoulder blade.

I lift my head. "I would be honoured."

I take his hand in the promenade position and we enter the ballroom. I curtsy and take the first three steps, twirl, and catch his hand again as he comes forward. I see myself in the mirror, smiling wide. I haven't tripped! There's Papa up in the top orchestral balcony, playing his violin, staring at us with wide eyes and … is that a bit of smile? See, Papa! Look at me now! We circle the great hall, weaving in and out with the other couples. In all the mirrors, even the one on the ceiling, I see myself smiling and moving like a lady, not tripping, not once.

I don't want the music to end. When it does, I curtsy and the page bows low, and I rush off straight into Mama's arms. She holds me close.

"Where were you earlier? I was so worried!" She hugs me harder. "Then I saw you dancing with that nice young page. See what I told you? So graceful! My graceful daughter!" I rest my cheek against her satin sleeve. I think, in Mama's eyes, I will always be graceful and never invisible.

Seven

Catharina

"A FINE INSTRUMENT, Johann." Herr Spiess holds Papa's new violin up to the candlelight and peers inside. It's a wonder I haven't yet spilled their coffee. I can't take my eyes off this violin. In the candlelight it's the colour of ... Mama's voice, the warm deep chestnut of it when she sings. If only I could touch it ... "Augsburg is fortunate to have such a maker as this Aman. What did you say his first name was?"

"Georg. Georg Aman. He just completed it last month. I received it for quite a decent price as well. He lowered—"

Papa quickly takes back the violin as Herr Spiess raises his shoulders, brings his hand to his mouth, and lets out an enormous sneeze.

Papa raises his eyebrows at me. Where is that Lumpi? I thought I'd shut her well away in the back room, but she must have somehow got loose. Or perhaps it was the dust on the landing. Herr Spiess takes a gulp of coffee and glares at me under his bushy eyebrows, as if I'm responsible for his sneeze. "Could you play a passage?" he asks Papa. "I'd love to hear how it sounds."

Papa nods and begins to play … *the* piece, the Concerto for Two Violins! I close my eyes and try to soak up each note as I did on the night when I first heard him try it. "Quite a sound, isn't it?" asks Papa, turning the violin in his hands so that it glints again.

"Glorious. The patrons at Carlsbad will be stunned. Speaking of Carlsbad, I must be off. Our five o'clock in the morning departure will come too soon, and I must give a proper farewell to my family. What news on the harpsichord?"

"The harpsichord! What an expense!" Papa laughs and carefully places his violin back in the case. I walk briskly to the table to take Herr Spiess's coffee cup. Perhaps just one touch, a brush of my knuckle against the wood.

"It seems the prince is willing to go to any expense to have it transported to Carlsbad," continues Papa, whose hand hovers too near the case. I'm sure he's almost about to close it. I draw my finger closer. "It will have its own special carriage, and servants to—"

"Achoo!" Herr Spiess lets rip another magnificent sneeze, and in that instant I brush my fingertip quickly against the wood of the scroll. Then I clatter away with the cup, almost spilling the coffee as I go. What I felt in that instant ... was a big, dark space somewhere at the back of my throat, big as the cathedral in Arnstadt, and the sound of rain on stained glass, and a sadness, the way I felt when looking in the darkening gazebo mirror and I saw the girl—not crying exactly, but holding something terrible inside ...

"... say farewell?" Papa's voice brings me back to the kitchen. He's closed the case and winks at Herr Spiess, who is rising from his chair. "I think our girl must still be back at the prince's ball, dancing." He gives a rare chuckle and smiles at me, and I soak up his smile as I would the sun. "I repeat—could you please fetch Mama and Tante Lena to say farewell to Herr Spiess?"

"Yes, Papa," I say, glad to run off.

"Well?" I turn back again at the sound of Papa's voice. "Do you have anything to say to our guest?" he asks.

"G-g-good ... morning, I mean, good evening, Herr S-S ... piess," I turn and flee to the sound of their laughter. I meant to say, "Goodbye, and have a most pleasant journey, Herr Spiess. And thank you for unwittingly letting me touch Papa's beautiful violin." But of course that didn't come out, and now Papa must surely think his daughter is a halfwit.

———

It will be dawn by the time Mama lets Papa go. His best performance clothes, and music, and several instruments, and extra handkerchiefs—everything he needs for a month or more—have all been packed into the waiting carriage that will drive him to the palace, where he'll join the prince's entourage on the long journey to Carlsbad. Papa looks sad to leave, but he must be a little excited as well. In Carlsbad, besides the healing warm waters, are grand hunting expeditions, and hotels and pavilions and rich counts and countesses with fancy clothes.

Papa gives Mama one last kiss. I blush and look away to see Tante Lena looking down at the street as well. Now if I were to someday marry the prince, he might kiss me just so, before leaving for Carlsbad ... except he would have me to take care of him and wouldn't be sick, and so he wouldn't need to travel and take Papa away and make Mama look so sad. She still hasn't cried, but she most likely will, once Papa is gone and she is alone in her room.

"Take good care of your mama." Papa gets down on one knee on the cobblestone and gives Wilhelm an embrace. "By the time I return, I expect you to have mastered the C-sharp minor prelude from the book I gave you. Do you promise?"

"Oh yes, Papa." Wilhelm nods solemnly.

I shiver and cross my arms. Even the end of May is chilly at dawn. I can't stop trembling and I think not just from the weather. What will Papa say when he comes to me? Maybe he will forget. The horses whinny as he says goodbye to Johann and Carl, and gives Tante Lena a tiny kiss on the cheek. He checks his pocket watch, then walks toward me quickly, as if he doesn't really have time but must fit me in, like a very small note at the end of a long passage of music.

"Be careful of that young page!" Papa says with a laugh. "I don't want to return and find my only daughter already married!"

"Johann, she's only twelve!" says Mama, looking a little less sombre.

The horses whinny again. "I must be off," he says, giving us a wave and getting in the carriage. "God keep you all until my return."

"God be with you, Johann," says Tante Lena to the departing carriage, her arm around Mama. We wave until we can no longer see the carriage, until it makes a turn onto Magdeburger Street. Papa, gone for a month or more. The steps I take from the landing to our apartments, two at a time, feel lighter, and I even try a little gavotte step on the top landing. When I reach the kitchen the others are gathered around the table, looking much gloomier than I am.

"But, Mama, who will give me my music lessons?" Wilhelm whines, rapping his fist on the table in a rhythm, trying to imitate Papa.

"You will just have to practise hard without lessons and impress Papa on his return." Mama sits in Papa's usual place and folds her hands tightly in front of her on the table. I thought she'd want to be alone to cry, but she must have swallowed it all. "Now," she continues, "I want no moping and laziness, just because Papa is away. Carl, wipe those tears right now. You must be brave for Papa, a little man. Stop slumping and yawning, Johann—"

"But it's so early in the morning and I'm hungry and sleepy," says Johann.

"Humph!" says Tante Lena. "We only just had bread and cheese and wurst with your papa before he left. You should have eaten more then, instead of complaining now."

But Mama has already sliced thick pieces of bread during Tante Lena's speech and now brings them to the table and takes Johann on her knee, kisses his chubby cheek. "Chores and practising and morning prayers before school, and school for Wilhelm, as usual," says Mama. "The busier we keep, the sooner he'll return—"

"But, Mama," Wilhelm asks, "perhaps just today I can miss school, in honour of Papa's departure and because we had to rise so dreadfully early?"

Mama shakes her head firmly. "School as usual, and after it, chores and practice and early to bed. Now, to the clavichord for prayers. Wilhelm will play for us in Papa's absence."

I'm happy that Mama won't be moping in her room for Papa. Of course she wouldn't. And maybe Papa has arranged for Herr Colm to bring her lilacs again in his absence. I skip all the way to the Latin school; Wilhelm for once has trouble keeping up. "Perfect, perfect, perfect, a month with Papa gone," I chant all the way home after I've dropped him off.

"Good morning, Mama!" I nearly shout, and she tells me to keep my voice lower because of Tante Lena napping. "It's a wonderful day," I whisper, taking a chair next to her at the table where she sits copying music.

"Oh? Why?" She takes a new sheet of paper, dips the fork-like rastrum in ink, wipes off the extra ink with a brush, and draws it across the page to make five new lines for the staff. It looks like … a fence by a meadow that one must climb over to find wild roses, or four roads side by side, leading off the page to … to … the place where the girl lives? In all the excitement of Papa's departure, I've forgotten about the girl with the big nose! Was that her in the cathedral when I touched the violin? I don't feel her sadness anymore—how can I when I have Mama sitting right next to me, and no Papa for a month at least!

"Well …" I dawdle with my answer, watch Mama make the graceful curve of a treble clef. "The weather is fine, and Tante Lena is napping—"

"Catharina Dorthea!" Mama scolds with a laugh, then sighs. "I wish I could so easily manage without Papa. No music! No rehearsals! No violin sound will drift into my dreams this night."

"I'll miss the music, too. But other things I won't miss—"

"Catharina!" says Mama in a very stern voice. "You mustn't ever speak that way about your papa. If he could hear you now, how hurt—"

"He wouldn't. He doesn't give me any notice. He … thinks I'm dim-witted." I've never spoken of Papa like this to Mama.

"Catharina Dorthea! How can you say such a thing!" She dribbles a bit of ink off a quarter note. Now she'll have to wait until it's dried and use the sharpening knife to erase it. I shouldn't have said anything in the first place. Mama hates making a mistake and hardly ever does, so I must have upset her terribly.

"He may seem a little more … focused on Wilhelm sometimes. But you have to understand how very little time he has, and of course it's very important that Wilhelm and the boys follow in his footsteps."

"Yes, Mama." I rise to get the broom and begin my chores. But I'm pressing it so hard into the floor that I think the bristles might break. "No! I don't understand!" The girl with the big nose would throw down her broom and stamp her foot on the floor. "Isn't it important that *I* follow in his footsteps, too?" she'd ask Mama. "Why does he pay more attention to Wilhelm and give him clavier and composition lessons and write books especially for him? Does he love Wilhelm more than me?" Questions that I've kept inside for so long are suddenly flung into the open by the girl, like a good, cool, salt breeze coming along on a muggy day to stir everything up. I stop sweeping and take a look at Mama. If I could only ask her, right now … I take a deep breath and open my mouth … but I can't. I sigh. Maybe not those questions, not yet. But another …

"Mama …"

"Yes?"

"Do you think … perhaps … we could sing a bit?" She'll probably be too busy.

"What song?"

"The one from the birthday concert … that Madame Monjou sang."

"Wasn't she wonderful?" Mama puts down her pen and stands and curtsies as if she's wearing a fancy gown, then sings the opening bars of "Today Is a Good Day." "It's such a difficult one," she continues, sitting back down. "I could never manage all those trills near the end."

She thinks I know nothing. I take a deep breath, stand, and sing the hard section with all of the trills, the one I worked on with Madame Monjou, then quickly sit down and bury my head in my arms.

Silence. And then I feel her fingers stroking my hair. "When …"

"After the concert. She taught me—Madame Monjou."

"We've always sung folk songs together … and hymns. Never your papa's difficult works. I must tell him—he needs to know this, to hear you. As soon as he returns—"

I lift my head. "It was just a surprise for you, Mama. A secret."

"But he can arrange vocal lessons for you. And a position, eventually ..."

"I'll tell him someday, I will—"

"Not someday. As soon as he returns." She laughs. "Can't you just see the expression on his face when he hears you trill? There's another piece—a duet for soprano and alto from last year's birthday cantata. Shall we try it? It must be up in his studio." She heads for the stairs and I follow along behind, laughing at her jumping two steps at a time in all her big skirts.

She heads straight for the glass cupboard behind his desk and begins to thumb through the compositions. "Ah!" she shouts, whipping off a piece from the stack. "Here it is! Just the thing for today!"

She opens the window and we hang over the sill, sing the joyful melody at the top of our lungs out to the street, until boys skipping school and dogs and women off to the market stop and look up at us and smile. Each time one of us makes a mistake, we stop and work at the bit until it's fixed, and then start from the beginning again and sometimes stop just to laugh and feel the breeze on our cheeks, and I lose track of the time in the sound of the notes and her laugh and the birds trilling with us in the blossoming cherry tree.

"Let's try it again!" Mama says when we're through. "We'll make fewer mistakes this time!" And we lean over the sill and begin the opening trill again.

"Heavens, what's all the ruckus about?" Tante Lena stands at the door in her old, brown dressing gown, rubbing her eyes, wearing the sourest frown.

"Oh, Lena, so sorry, it must be time for your coffee and cake." Mama rushes over to the door.

"Such hilarity so soon after the master's absence. I'm surprised at you, Maria Barbara. And in his private studio, too."

"Catharina and I were just … practising … some music," says Mama quietly, winking at me behind Tante's back. "Would you like a tray brought up to your room?"

"If it isn't too much trouble," says Tante Lena, shuffling up the stairs. "It's the back today. Such aches."

In the kitchen, Mama places a spare sheet of paper, the rastrum, and the quill in front of me. "You must learn to copy what you just sang. It's good training." She shows me how to hold the rastrum's wooden handle and how to dip it in ink without overloading the ink channels. "These will make the lines of the staff," she points to the five brass nibs at the end of it. "Practise eight staves, all the way down the page, and then I'll show you the treble clef. You must draw the rastrum steadily and firmly. Otherwise the lines won't be straight."

I've seen Mama draw the rastrum a hundred times. It should be easy. I take a deep breath, dip it in the ink, brush off the excess, and draw. Five lines, wavery with my trembling. I look over at Mama.

"It's natural for your first staff to be crooked," she says. "Practise!"

"Why do the second and third lines look slightly closer together than the rest?"

"Oh, don't worry about that, it's just the way Papa's rastrum was cut."

I try the next and the next, and after half a page of crooked staves, I begin a letter:

May 30, 1720

Dear Girl,

I wanted you to see my crooked attempts to make staves. It's rather tedious work. I'd rather

*sing music than copy it! Oh, if only you could
have heard the wonderful music that Mama
and I just sang together! But I also wanted to
thank you for asking those questions, even if I
didn't have the courage to ask them of Mama
today. It made me feel so much better, just to
hear them asked. It felt as if someone were
cutting the tight strings of a small parcel, one
by one ... Now, I must get back to copying.*

Yours,
Catharina

Hannah

"Try the passage again, thinking about how the
rhythm shows which notes are important," says
Mr. Dekker, crossing one leg over the other and
bending down to stroke Penny. He's the coolest
teacher—but today is one of those days when I
want Mom sitting in that chair. "Bach gave so little
information about expression—how loud or soft
to play, how long or short to hold a note—on the
actual music, so you have to find his clues in the
form—repeated phrases, new beginnings, curious

turns—and in the rhythm and harmony." Penny escapes his hand and comes to rub against my leg, purring. Mr. Dekker laughs. "It looks like the Princess Penny has decided to be your friend today. Do you mind her there while you play?"

I shake my head. I'm trying to think about the passage of Bach, and how to express it in the rhythm. I think about finding clues—how would Bach have played it? If only I could listen to him play it as I used to listen to Mom—as I washed the dishes or did my homework or in that groggy space just before sleep. I lift my violin to my chin and try to hear the passage in my head. The way she always played it. The numb ache I felt after she died, how alone I feel, even when there are other people around, as if there's no one in the world who will ever understand.

"Hannah? Are you going to play?" Mr. Dekker's looking at me strangely.

I glance in the mirror and order the girl in there to lift her bow and place it on the string. In that instant—the moment my bow touches the string to make a sound—I see in the mirror the girl from the ball, pulling open a door. And then, rushing out of that room, the Bach Double so clear, played by an orchestra and Mom's violin playing the solo—clear and warm as if it's right next to me. The music washes some of the ache away, as if someone's finally understood how I felt. I dig my bow into the string and play along with the rhythm that feels so clearly set out before me.

"There it is, Hannah! Bravo!" And even as Mr. Dekker shouts these words that I've been longing to hear ever since I started taking from him, his voice is fading and I can barely catch his next words. "Try the whole passage now, from letter A ..."

It's kind of like when I was playing at Marie's party. I had to fit into the rhythm of the dance, to the people moving in front of me, and I couldn't think about how scared I was or that I might make a mistake. And now, there's this orchestra playing, and the girl with such a big grin, swaying to the music that pours out of the room. I close my eyes and let those clear, sure notes take over, right to the end of the passage.

"... did it again, Hannah!" Mr. Dekker's words come in from far away and he swings into focus as the girl in the mirror becomes me again. He puts his violin in his case and scoops up Penny. "Is Princess Penny your secret? I think Johann Sebastian himself would have been proud of that passage from his concerto." His words get gradually louder, as if someone is turning up the volume. "You must have practised hard this week. What did you do?"

I feel dizzy, and look down at my violin. Just my plain old three-quarters size with the scratches and the pegs that won't stay in place. But it was Mom's violin that I heard, Mom's violin that's been so quiet for so long. And where did the girl come from?

"Hannah?" Mr. Dekker looks at me curiously.

"Um, I—I ... went to a fiddle party and learned 'St. Anne's Reel.'"

He laughs. "Well, carry on—you've been improving by leaps and bounds, especially today." He pauses for a minute. "Say ... for that assembly at school, you said you were playing 'Humoresque'? Why don't you play the Bach Double? I think you're ready, and it would be good practice for your Book 4 graduation recital in June. When is it—the assembly, I mean?"

The Bach Double for Melissa and the Town Girls? I'll fall off the roller coaster for sure. "Um ... it's actually in three weeks, which is way too soon, don't you think?"

He laughs. "The way you played it today? It'll be wonderful."

"Who'll play the first part?"

141

He loosens his bow. I'm his last student on Mondays, and it looks as if today he doesn't have to rush off to symphony rehearsal. "I know! Bridget! It will be perfect review for her, and she can stay after her lesson and go over the part with you ... starting next week."

Bridget the Perfect? "But she has ballet. And will she want to drive all the way out to Clear Lake?"

"Oh, her mother encourages these kinds of things, doesn't mind her missing school and all that, drives her anywhere. I'll give them a call and let you know, okay?" He really thinks I can do it.

"Do I have to play it from memory?"

"Of course!" He studies me closely. "Now don't worry. You need to have more confidence in your own playing. Just get up there and sing the part on your violin. It'll be great."

I guess I'm in for it. I can't say no to Mr. Dekker. The Bach Double for Clear Lake Elementary School. I'd rather play for a huge dark auditorium full of strangers. It would be less scary. I loosen my bow and wipe my violin and follow him down the hallway to the kitchen. He opens the cupboard and gets out a needle for Penny's diabetes shot.

"How old is Penny?" I ask, putting on my boots.

"Good question. I don't know. She already seemed pretty old when I found her in the neighbourhood fifteen years ago. I put up signs and no one ever claimed her, so she just stayed on." He fills Penny's bowl, takes her by the scruff of the neck while she's eating, and gives her the shot.

I wind my scarf around my neck. "What's the name of her new painting?" I point to the flowers above Penny's dish.

He laughs. "Penny loves Van Gogh. This one is called *Irises*. Who knows? Maybe she's old enough to have seen this painted by the master himself!" He gives me a wink and walks with me through the living room.

I look at my watch. "Yikes! I have to catch my bus."

He opens the door. "I'll give you a call about Bridget and the Bach Double. Oh, and Hannah, one more thing—"

"What?"

"I should have mentioned this before. We should start thinking about moving you up to a full-size violin pretty soon."

A blast of wind hits my face, and I almost lose my balance on the stair. All of a sudden I want so badly to tell him about Mom's violin, about the girl opening the door and that sound rushing out. "It was that sound I heard during my lesson—that's what helped me to play so well," I want to tell him, and then about the way Dad keeps it locked in a closet, how I snuck into his room to try it out and almost fainted, the smell of the wood and Mom's lotion and ... well, just everything. But mostly I want to tell him about how much I want to play it. I open my mouth, but all that comes out is "I'll ... have to ask my dad. Bye." I turn away and begin to run down the sidewalk to the bus depot, the icy wind in my face.

Why didn't I say anything? Usually I can blab on and on, and today, just when I really want to talk, I have to go and turn mute. My case bangs against my leg with each step. That sound—the sound of Mom's violin—how did I hear it, and did I just imagine the girl opening that door, or ...

"It's a beautiful sound, isn't it?" asks the girl, running beside me wearing all her big skirts and a heavy fur coat. She makes clouds with her breath as we run. "What is it like to play?"

"You've never played it?"

"Of course not! Only Papa and his men play the violin!"

I think of Mom playing in the symphony. "Why? That seems to me like an extremely dumb rule."

144

She sighs. "Well, it's not a rule, exactly. It's just the way things are." She glances down at my case and touches it. "You're so lucky to play …"

I push open the big double doors into the light and clang of the bus depot. I remember the way it was in the lesson when I got the Bach Double right and feel a warmth run right up my gut. "You're right! I am lucky!" I shout to her and the people waiting in line for tickets, but when I turn to look for her smile, she's disappeared. There's only Peppermint Woman looking at me disapprovingly, as if I've gone completely crazy. But I don't care. I get in line behind her, trying to keep the sound of Mom's violin in my head, planning a way to get it.

Eight

Hannah

"A CERTAIN MEMBER of our class is in BIG trouble," I overhear Melissa half whisper to the girls gathered around her desk. They all start to giggle and whisper and point to me. I duck my head behind Hilary the Head Girl and pretend to read. Melissa must have squealed about the library. Or maybe she's just trying to give me a scare.

"Oh, really, who?" asks Tracy, flipping her blond hair away from her face and smirking at me.

"I'll give you a hint," says Melissa. "She lives in a house that's HAUNTED." They all fall into giggles. If only Ms. Lockport hadn't driven by and offered me a ride. I'd rather be fighting the blizzard than stuck in here. I could just leave the classroom—go out into the hall and get a drink of water. I could hide in the washroom until the bell. But that would look dumb. It's too late now—I'm stranded.

"Next clue." Melissa snaps her gum. "She has a very WEIRD dad. In fact, he's so weird that he doesn't even know how to drive. Back in the fall I saw him WALK home from the store pulling a wagon for groceries." She bursts out laughing. Some of the other kids start drifting into the classroom. Please, please, Mr. Peters, walk in early.

"And why is this person in such big trouble?" asks Brianne in a flat voice, as if Melissa wrote out the script for her ahead of time and she's just reading a line.

"Well," Melissa says, leaning back in her chair and looking up at the circle around her. "Another very weird thing about her is that she hangs around in the LIBRARY—"

She's interrupted by the bell. Mr. Peters walks into the room and begins to make notes on the board. Under the heading *Principal* he writes *Hannah*. I guess it's better than if he announced it out loud, but on the other hand, it's there for everyone to see for the whole day. The entire class turns around and stares. If only I could press Delete on Melissa's smirk.

"Okay, class, no need to stare," says Mr. Peters. "Open your books for silent reading." I'm glad we don't have to do math. Now I can just sit here pretending to read. Dad will be so upset when he

147

finds out that I'm in trouble. Is being in the library at noon so bad? In Toronto I spent every noon hour there—a bunch of us did—as librarian assistants. I loved helping to check out the books and printing out labels and stuff on the computer.

The time until lunch drags by. Doesn't Mr. Peters see Melissa passing notes, right under his eyes? She drops one, and before I can stop myself I swoop it up off the floor. "Dear Trace, She doesn't even wear makeup!! She needs SOMETHING for that nose. A nose ring?? M. P.S. The usual Plan A after school if it stops blizzarding."

Melissa sees me tuck it into my pocket. You never know when you'll need evidence. When the noon bell finally goes, I'm the first to get out of the classroom. I bet Melissa and the Town Girls are just dying to tease me about it, but I'm not going to give them the chance. I sprint down the hallway and arrive breathless in the office.

"No running in the halls, Hannah," says Ms. Lockport, without the winning smile. "We don't want to add to your little list of troubles, do we?" She glances at the calendar. "So, your assembly performance is in three weeks? Are you ready?"

"Not really," I say. She already asked me this yesterday, on the way to my lesson. All I want is to get this over with. Mr. Franckowiak is going to be in trouble, too, all because of me.

"I'm sure everything will work out fine. Now, are you ready to see Mr. Griggs?"

"Ready as I'll ever be." I've met him before, but that was with Dad. How will I keep Mr. Franckowiak out of trouble? He could lose his job.

Mr. Griggs is peeling an orange as I walk in, and some juice squirts on his glasses. He takes a tissue and wipes them as if this happens all the time. There are rumours that he's almost about to retire, and that Ms. Lockport wants her husband to get the job so that they can move to Clear Lake and be closer to her old mother.

"Well, well ... Hannah." He pops an orange section into his mouth and shuffles some papers on his desk. "How is school?"

Why doesn't he just get to the point? "It's ... um ... fine, I guess."

"A bit different from Toronto, I suppose."

"A lot different, actually. My school in Toronto was way bigger, and there were way more kids from different backgrounds, and I was in French immersion, but the gym wasn't nearly as nice, and the number of kids in the classes was a lot—"

"But some things are the same ... like rules that

149

every student must follow for the school to function in an orderly way."

"But some of them seem like such extremely dumb rules, especially the library one!" I almost shout. "In Toronto we got to stay in the library every noon hour, as librarian's assistants, and I learned so much—"

"Hannah, this isn't your school in Toronto." He's stopped eating his orange but is shredding the tissue. "I ask you to please keep your voice down and try not to make an entire speech every time I ask you to speak." He glances at his watch. "A student has informed me that you were seen leaving the library at noon hour. Is this true?"

I nod slowly. "Another thing about my old school was that it wasn't cool to snitch on other people, even if they weren't friends." Oops. Why can't I just keep quiet? It's as if I'm rolling down a hill and can't stop.

"Hannah! Every remark like that is just getting you deeper into trouble. Do you understand?" I manage to nod without saying anything. "How did you get in?"

"It was unlocked."

"And what were you doing?"

"I was just … um … just …"

"Yes?"

"I was just reading this book." I hold up Hilary the Head Girl hopefully. "But as I was saying, what's so bad about that? It's not as if I was hurting anyone ..."

His face is turning red. "It was strictly against the rules outlined very clearly on the first day of school."

How can I tell him that I'd much rather be sitting by the heating vent in the warm darkness listening to music and reading than standing by myself on the playground? I think of the last time I was there, when Mr Franckowiak played "The Girl with the Flaxen Hair" and it made me think of summer and Mom and the corn maze ... stop. "All I can say is that it's a rule I don't understand at all!" My voice is so loud. I can't help it.

"Hannah Waters, I ask you to please keep your voice down when talking to me." His tone is angry and as pinched as a too-tight jacket. "I'm sure it's going to take time for you to adjust to our school." He's trying hard to keep his temper under control. "We simply don't have the budget to keep the library supervised at noon. And if we allow you in there, all the other kids will want to as well ..."

Budget. That's a word I've heard before. Mom in the symphony, Dad at the university—they were always talking about budget cuts. I feel a little sorry for saying so much.

He clears his throat. "For punishment ... you will stay after school, beginning today and for a whole week, and make sure all the whiteboards are absolutely spotless. Now ... the library shouldn't have been open. Was there somebody else in there besides you?"

Here it comes. Now what will I do? How can I tattle like Melissa? What if Mr. Franckowiak loses his job? But I can't lie. It'll just make things worse. "Mr. Griggs," I say, pushing up my glasses, "I can't say anything on the grounds that it may incriminate a friend."

I look up at him and hope to see a smile play around the corners of his mouth, but he just shuffles his papers and looks displeased and throws away his orange peel. "I see ... so there was someone there. And was he, perhaps, playing the piano?"

I say nothing.

"It looks as though I'm going to have to have a talk with our custodian."

"Oh ... Mr. Griggs ... please don't—"

"You've said quite enough already, Hannah. You may go to your room now for lunch, and afterwards, the playground." He looks out the window at the clearing sky. "The blizzard has finished. Report to the office after school for your detention. Ms. Lockport will phone your father to tell him you'll be late."

"But Mr.—"

"That will be all. And in the future, I suggest that you show a little more respect for your principal, your school, and its rules." He opens the door to let me out and closes it firmly behind me.

⁂

"Think on the bright side," I say, as I swipe a whole row of fractions clean. "What's the worst that could happen?"

"Mr. Franckowiak could get fired, and all because of you," answers the girl in the window with the streetlight earrings.

"Right." There's something very satisfying about erasing a bunch of math. "But on the bright side, if he gets fired—"

"He'll have to go on welfare, and all because of you."

"No, he'll be able to start a new career as a concert pianist, and travel the world and make millions of dollars. That's what he should do anyway, not take care of this old school."

"How's he going to do that?"

"Oh, Dad can help him. He can contact Mom's old friends in Toronto and ..."

I look at the clock—almost four. I put down the brush and run down the hallway and into the office. Ms. Lockport is straightening her pink beret and scarf in a handheld mirror.

"Running in the halls again, Hannah? Aren't you in enough trouble already?"

"Is Mr. Franckowiak done with Mr. Griggs yet?"

"Yes, as a matter of fact," she says, pulling on her gloves, which are pink, of course. "He just left. He ... well, let's just say he was a little upset. He was walking home, as usual. Mr. Griggs left for a meeting at the high school. Mrs. Smith, the Grade 1 teacher, is working late and will lock up after you're done. Hannah! No running in the halls!"

I'm already tearing down the hall, slip-sliding in my sock feet, toward the entrance Mr. F. would take to go home. A blast of cold wind hits my face as I push open the door. Snow swirling diamonds and clanging swings and no Mr. Franckowiak. I have to tell him I'm sorry. I race back to check the last room, the music room, which luckily doesn't need anything because today wasn't music day.

By the time I'm dressed in all my winter clothes

and running down the path out of the schoolyard, it's almost dark, and the snow is that spooky blue that would give me a delicious shiver any other day. Where would he be by now? I think he lives down by the tracks somewhere, on the far end of town. I tear out of the schoolyard and through a back alley, trying to remember the way I've seen him walk.

I'm almost to the corner of the park when I see the silhouette of a cluster of kids up on the bleachers, on the end part that sticks out beyond the backstop. They're screaming and laughing and throwing snowballs. I run toward them. I should really be running away from them—this looks like trouble and I'm in enough already—but I'm sure it's the fastest way to catch up to Mr. Franckowiak.

Melissa spots me first. "Well, if it isn't Hannah Waters out from detention, just in time to help." She packs a snowball, then flings her blue velvet scarf away from her face and throws hard, screaming, "Take that, Mr. Quack!!" I remember her note ... *Plan A by the bleachers*. Everyone's quacking like ducks and pelting piles of snowballs. I look at their target—Mr. Franckowiak, walking slowly down the path with his head down and his hands in his pockets. I recognize his fur hat.

"Don't just stand there," says Melissa. "Make yourself useful. The last girl to hit Mr. Quack before he's out of reach for five nights in a row"—she glances over at Jeremy and Ben— "gets to go to the dance at the high school with ... er ... someone really great." She looks at me and flashes her braces. "Listen, this is your last chance. Make me a pile of snowballs and you can walk home with us, have another test—"

"NO!" I scream and run out to the ball diamond, to where the pitcher's mound should be, and jump in all directions, trying to block the shots from hitting Mr. Franckowiak. Splat! One hits me square in the glasses. They all start laughing, and someone, I think it's Melissa, yells, "Hit Hannah Banana instead of Quack!"

I scream at the top of my lungs, "What has he ever done to you?" Another snowball splats in my face and more laughter bursts from the stands.

"Hannah?" says Mr. Franckowiak's soft voice behind me. "Come with me." I take one last look at the crowd and follow him slowly down the path. "Don't turn around," he says, as a few stray snowballs hit our backs. "Just keep on walking. Slowly. It's not so bad, really."

"Do they do this every day?"

He nods. "For the past week or so."

"Why don't you walk a different way?"

"Let a bunch of kids scare me off? Never."

"But why you? What have you ever done to them?"

He laughs. "It gives them something to do. It makes them feel powerful, up there high in the stands, hitting a target. In the war ..."

His voice trails off and his pace picks up so that I have to jog to keep up to him. He stops suddenly and turns around. "I've grown somewhat accustomed to those snowballs, but thank you for standing up for me. Thank you."

His face looks ghostly pale in the moonlight, and sad, as if he's holding secrets too terrible to ever tell. I wonder why he came all the way to a lame old town like Clear Lake in the first place. If I were him, I never would've come near this place. He should have gone to Toronto.

I'm bursting with my question. "Did Mr. Griggs ... um ... fire you?"

He laughs. "You do have an imagination, don't you? That's good. Musicians need an imagination. No, he didn't fire me, only ..." He turns back around and starts walking again.

"Only what?"

"He suspended my piano privileges in the library. Says it was a breach of trust for me to let you in. So there'll be no more Bartók in the library at noon hours—"

"I'm sorry! It's all my fault. Melissa told on me, but I didn't say anything about you to Mr. Griggs. But if I hadn't come in that day—"

"Fiddlesticks," he says. "I knew perfectly well you weren't supposed to be in there. I could have told you to leave."

"I could have left on my own. Now where will you play?"

"Oh, I'll find a way."

"I'll help you. I promise." We've stopped at the place where the path branches into two. It's so quiet and dark. "I guess I should go," I say, pulling my scarf over my face. It's soaked and stiff with snow-balls that have melted and then frozen again. "My dad'll be worried."

"Goodbye, Hannah, and remember, I'm playing for you in the assembly. 'Humoresque.'"

"I was going to tell you. Mr. Dekker just changed it to the Bach Double. Will you still play for that?"

He smiles. "Nothing could make me happier."

I trudge home through the snow, trying to figure out how I can help Mr. F. find a piano. Melissa takes piano lessons, but I'd never try to work something out with her. A full moon is rising over the Lutheran church. Maybe there's a piano in there? I'll ask Dad for help, even though I'm dreading what he'll say about my detention. I've never been in trouble like this before. And somehow I have to tell him about the bigger violin, too. I can hear the scrape of his shovel on the driveway before I even reach the house.

"Dad!" I yell at him from behind, and he jumps and turns around. I can just hear Mom saying, "It's Gerhard, shifting in from the Planet of Snow to the Planet of Hannah in Trouble."

"Hannah!" he says, throwing down the shovel. "I heard all about your trouble in school from Ms. Lockport. That woman knows how to talk!" He rubs his ears. "Hanging around in the library, were you?"

I nod and draw my foot through the snow. Here it comes.

"I think I heard more about it than I'll ever need to know, so you don't need to explain anything."

"But ... but I disobeyed the rules ..."

"Your detention is punishment enough for that." He starts walking toward the house and I follow. "Imagine!" he says, and laughs a deep laugh I haven't heard for a long time. "Punished for being in the library! I'd have received an awful lot of detentions if that was against the rules when I was in school." He laughs again, another deep one. "Chip off the old block, eh?"

"But the principal won't let Mr. F. play in the library anymore. And it's all my fault. I told him I'd try to help. But where will we find a piano?"

"You're forgetting that we have one! And a grand one at that!"

Of course! How could I have forgotten about the piano in Ontario? "Do you think Uncle Ted and Aunt Ruth will mind transporting it all the way out here? It would be perfect in the living room, with the new floor. And Mr. F. can come over to our place to practise and give lessons! Yes! I'll call Uncle Ted tonight." I dance a little jig on the driveway. "Thanks, Dad!"

Maybe it won't be so hard to ask him about the violin after all. Maybe I'll go straight ahead and ask for Mom's. "What's for supper?" I ask, even though I already know what it'll be.

"I'll give you a clue," he says with another laugh. "Tomatoey, cheesey, lots of long slithery things—"

"Dad!" I laugh.

"But wait!" he says. "I made something else. A surprise. Follow me." He leads me around the corner of the house to the backyard.

There, in the moonlight, shines a silvery maze of ice and snow. The walls are mostly higher than my head, and there are all kinds of twists and turns and corners and dead ends running the whole length of the yard.

Dad pushes up his glasses. "Do you like it?" he asks softly.

I can't say anything for a bit. "Like it? Oh, Dad, it's beautiful ... when?"

"Oh" —he kicks some snow—"there was all that snow from the blizzard, and when I heard about your trouble after lunch I figured you'd need something ... We can try it out after supper, okay? It will be fun, with the full moon."

I think about the Corn Maze and I'm almost about to say, "If only Mom were here," but stop myself just in time and give him a bear hug instead. "Thanks, Dad," I say, "it's a-*maz*-ing!"

Catharina

I slip out of Papa's studio, where I've been practising trills, and sing a few scales as I make my way down to the landing, which I must dust. I can't keep from singing ever since Mama and I sang the duet

161

together. And tonight she and I will walk through the maze! Mama herself came up with the idea last night when she looked out the window and saw that it would be a full moon tonight. I pretend that I'm Madame Monjou and hold the top note of the scale extra long, then stand at the head of the stairs and bow to the audience of Latin school boys who can't stop clapping. "Bravo!" they shout. "We must have another song!" I smile sweetly and launch into another—

"What in heaven's name are you doing?" Tante Lena steadies her thin hand on the banister. Now I've done it! Gone and almost bumped my aunt off the stairs.

"I'm sorry, Tante—"

"Never mind your apologies. Such an odd girl. Traipsing all over the house with your head in the clouds, singing nonsense at the top of your lungs. Watch where you're going next time." She continues up the stairs. "Better go to the kitchen. Your mama's in a state, with finally a letter from your poor over-worked papa."

I fly down the stairs. "A letter from Papa!" I say, running into the kitchen. Mama has been anxiously waiting for a letter for three weeks, ever since Papa's departure.

Mama just nods and smiles and looks up briefly from the letter. I sit quietly watching and won't interrupt, although I'm bursting with questions. When did the letter arrive? How is Carlsbad? When will … he be arriving home? Perhaps the prince is now dreadfully ill and they'll have to stay for another month.

Mama's face is flushed and she laughs out loud as she reads. "Listen, Catharina," she says, and clears her throat.

> "The prince's health has improved considerably even in the few days since we've arrived. Since even the fastest private mail coach is unacceptably slow (and you will only be receiving this when it is almost time for me to come home) I want to take this opportunity to inform you, my dearest wife, that if he continues to improve in this way, we should be arriving home no later than July 10 …"

"But that's …" I rapidly calculate the days in my head. "That's in one week!" I try to hide the dismay in my voice.

"Yes!" Mama says. "The time has really gone very quickly, hasn't it? And it's strange to hear about the first two days when he's almost about to arrive home, thanks to our horribly slow mail coaches, even if they are private. But listen, here's a funny account of the prince hunting for deer …"

I swallow a lump in my throat and pretend I'm listening and trace my finger over the grain of the wood in the table. Only a week left! The time has gone too fast. Each day my voice has been getting stronger in morning prayers, until yesterday Mama said again that she would most certainly talk to Papa about having my voice trained! Trained, like a professional, like Madame Monjou!

Each day the sun has risen into a clear blue sky. A few weeks ago, Mama suggested an outing by the river. We stowed bread and cheese and a fig cake in a basket, and even Tante Lena found herself well enough to come along. Lise held an umbrella for her while she napped on a little portable bed we'd brought for her. Carl and Johann chased Wilhelm until he climbed into an old apple tree and then crashed down from one of the branches. I was tempted to call him "Clumsy Will" but held my tongue. He made a big fuss, of course, but he only scraped his elbow. I spread my skirts out on the ground rug with Mama napping peacefully beside me. I scooped up a handful of the moist earth and wished that I could hold time like that in my hand, keep it from moving like the current of the river below me, stay like that, always, Mama's steady breathing, the laughter of the boys, Mama chuckling in her sleep …

"… and soon I will have the pleasure of seeing your loveliness again. Your Johann."

Mama folds the letter and tucks it in her pocket. "Are you ready for the maze?" she asks, sweeping the hearth, although I swept it clean as a cloud only an hour ago.

"Ready? It feels as if I've been waiting for this all my life." I try to forget that Papa is coming home soon. Tonight, I'll hold time tight in my fist, and nothing will take it away from Mama and me.

Herr Colm meets us at the palace gates and escorts us to the entrance of the maze. "Frau Bach, I am quite concerned about this excursion. Perhaps you'd like to reconsider and take a cup of chocolate with Her Highness Mother instead—"

Mama laughs and looks at me. "My daughter would never forgive me if I bowed out now.

Besides, there's really nothing to be afraid of. It's not as if wild animals lurk in the centre of the maze!"

"Nevertheless, I will sit here on this bench at the entrance until your return. You could become lost," says Herr Colm, twisting his hands. "I'll sit here and think about my decision."

"What decision?" asks Mama.

"Oh … nothing … nothing of your concern right now, Frau Bach." The moon lights the creases on his forehead. He looks as though he would like nothing better than to tell Mama all about his decision. "If you could know of my trouble, how ill I've been ever since the birthday concert, unable to copy a note, and the court surgeon gone with the prince to Carlsbad."

"Is there no other doctor in all of Cöthen?" Mama looks concerned. I admire her patience, listening to old Herr Colm when the maze is splashing in moonlight, calling to us. I can almost hear the fountain. Will Herr Colm never let us go?

He shakes his head. "Tomorrow I must travel all the way to Zerbst. But I'm keeping you from the maze." He sits on the bench.

"Farewell!" says Mama, as if we're about to set out on a long journey, and leads the way into the maze.

It's such a warm evening. The air is moist and has curled the small hairs at the back of Mama's neck. I run a little to catch up to her. She holds out her hand, and I take it as if I were still a little girl. "It won't be hard to get through this! You know the way so well, Mama," I say.

"I've been through a few times," she says. "But it's almost as if the moon is leading the way. Do you feel it?"

I nod. "And listen," I say, as we round a corner, "do you hear the fountain? That's what helped Wilhelm and me. We listened our way in."

"But if you listened your way in, how did you get out?"

I remember the glazed look in Wilhelm's eyes, the heat of the sun, how we kept making wrong turns and running into dead ends, how the double concerto led me out. We round another corner—we haven't had one dead end. Now is the time to tell Mama about that strange day. "Will you believe me when I tell you … that music led us out? I heard it plain as day—the second solo part from Papa's Concerto for Two Violins."

"Papa must have been playing it at the other end," she says flatly.

"Did he say?"

167

She frowns a little. "No, but who else could have been playing?" She laughs a little. "Certainly not Herr Spiess! Then sneezing as well as music would have led you out!"

"But it sounded different from Papa. Some of the notes weren't in tune. Mama?" I give her hand a squeeze as we turn the corner. What has happened to all the dead ends?

"Yes," she says softly. She lifts her skirts and jumps over a pool of moonlight as if it's water.

"I think … it was … a girl … the one who's not afraid … my friend … I know it sounds strange but I can't explain anything more than that." I take a deep breath and skip over the moonlight pool, too, and laugh as I catch Mama's hand on the other side.

Mama looks up at the moon. "I've noticed before … there's a certain quality to this maze … is it something in the air? It makes you believe anything could happen in here, even imaginary friends playing the violin."

"But she's not imaginary!" I give her hand a tug and pull us around the next corner. "I mean … at certain times she feels more real than anything. Here's the centre!"

"It's just as lovely as I remember, lovelier all lit

by the moon," Mama says, walking to the miniature pool.

I run to the lilac hedge, hoping to pluck some blossoms for Mama, but most of them are gone; only a few withered purple ones, brown around the edges, droop from the hedges. "You should have seen the lilacs before! So full, just heaps of them. Their scent led us in along with the sound of the fountain. I wanted to pick some for you."

"They're always finished by the beginning of July," says Mama, not moving from her bench by the pool and the fountain. "But see over there by the gazebo are beautiful pink roses. Can you smell them?"

I wrinkle my nose. "They're too sweet. I much prefer lilacs." I turn around and slowly walk to the miniature gazebo with the mirror.

There's nothing unusual about my reflection, just my cheeks white in the moonlight, the unruly hair escaping from my cap. "Hello," I whisper, "have you ever walked a maze with your mama? It's great fun."

She nods and smiles. I can see the back of Mama in the mirror. She's sitting quietly by the pool. She can sense, somehow, that I need to be alone.

"Do … you have any friends?" I whisper, and feel my heart beat faster, somewhere up in my forehead.

Mama in the mirror shifts on the bench.

"Your mama is your friend? So is mine. She's my best friend in the world. I ... I love her more than anyone else."

She looks as if she might cry, as I felt when I touched Papa's violin. I shiver as a cloud passes over the moon, turning my reflection in the mirror to night, and there's a frost deep inside me, so cold, the bitterest winter—snow and ice and stars that could break if I touched them. The cloud passes. I look anxiously into the mirror. Goosebumps on my arm. And Mama has disappeared from the bench by the pond.

"Mama! Where are you?" I scream, turning away from the mirror.

"Right here," she whispers, holding the entrance pillar of the gazebo. "Shh, Catharina, you'll have Herr Colm coming in after us. But ... what's wrong?" She touches my cheek.

"I was so frightened," I say, shivering and holding her tight as if I'll never let her go.

"Shh, shh, you'll be fine, just fine. One minute you were in the gazebo playing your game in the mirror, the next you were screaming my name—"

"Mama, you ... won't ever ... leave ... will you?"

She laughs and gently pulls herself away from me. "Like Papa left for Carlsbad? I don't think

170

there's much danger of the prince hiring me on and taking me away. Can you picture it—Maria Barbara Bach, official court copyist? But look at the moon! It's lighting our way back through the maze!"

Mama's right. How can I be unhappy on such a night? "I'll race you back to the entrance!" I shout, hopping over a pool of moonlight and starting back to the maze.

"Yes!" she shouts and laughs and passes me at the first turn. "But watch out, because your mama's quicker than she looks!"

"And your daughter's quicker than she looks," I say, passing her and making a sharp turn to avoid a dead end. I start to laugh and can't stop as I run, even though Mama passes me again, doubling over in laughter as she runs.

I'm still laughing until my stomach hurts as I feel myself nearing the end of the maze. I tag Mama as I pass, shouting, "It looks as if the daughter will win!" I push just ahead of her at the entrance, and we both collapse onto the wet grass.

Mama holds her stomach, heaving with laughter. "I haven't had so much fun in a long time," she squeezes out between breaths. "Oh, good evening, Herr Colm."

I look up and see him staring at us with his mouth wide open. "Do you think the Princess Agnes would still want us in for that cup of chocolate?" I ask in my primmest voice, and we collapse in the grass again, our laughter sailing up to the moon.

Nine

Catharina

"Papa told me to take care of you," says Wilhelm to Mama the next morning at breakfast, "so why was Catharina allowed to go with you through the maze last night?" He jabs his fork into a slice of wurst.

"Because it was a particular expedition that Catharina and I planned some time ago," says Mama, the corners of her mouth twitching in a smile. I almost start to laugh every time I think of the grass and the maze and the moon and Herr Colm's shocked expression.

"Goodness, Maria Barbara, you haven't eaten a thing," says Tante Lena, tapping Mama's empty plate. "Don't tell me this foolish late-night traipsing through a maze has ruined your appetite."

Mama shakes her head but still takes nothing from her plate. "Carl, don't take such a big mouthful of cheese. Papa will be home in seven days and will expect you to behave like a little man."

"He's going to be impressed by the C-sharp minor prelude," says Wilhelm. "And I even have a surprise to show him, something that I've composed myself."

Mama nods. "We must all think of something we can give Papa. He'll be so tired on returning from his long journey. Right after prayers, I'll begin some copying."

But after prayers, she heads up to her room.

"Is something the matter, Mama?" I call up the stairs after her.

"Nothing. Perhaps Lena is right, after all. I'm not used to late-night mazes and need some rest. Now go on and make sure Wilhelm gets to school on time."

The boys at the door sing in four parts their usual insults as we near the gate. After leaving Wilhelm, I walk away with "Clumsy Catharina" sung at my back by those rascals. One day ... one day I'll sing something back. "Snails! Snails! All of you are snails!" I'll sing with my new morning prayers voice, straight to their faces, and they'll never dare to insult me again.

The apartment is silent when I arrive home. Tante Lena is staring at her needlework in the sitting room. "Where is Mama?" I ask. Her needle-point rose looks the same as it did yesterday, and the coffee beside her sits untouched.

"She's in her room. I suggest you don't disturb her. I think you've tired her enough already, what with last night's adventure."

"But Mama's never tired!"

"Well, she is now, as I am." She rises very slowly from the chair. "I'm going to retire to my room. I suggest you make yourself useful and see that the younger boys aren't into mischief. And Lise will need help with dinner and the evening meal, of course."

She walks off, quite energetically it seems to me.

I check on Johann and Carl, who are playing quietly with a wooden puzzle. I pace through the rooms. What can be wrong with Mama? She was perfectly fine last night, laughing and talking all the way home from the palace. Could she have caught a cold? But the air was warm. I don't dare sneak up to her room to ask. I'd have to go past Tante Lena's room first, and she'd hear me right away and scold me for disobeying.

I spend the afternoon making staves and eighth notes and singing the song Madame Monjou sang at the prince's birthday, and helping Lise peel the potatoes for supper. Mama says I've actually become very adept at copying in a very short time, and means to talk to Papa about it as well as the voice training. Poor Papa won't know what to think when he arrives home—a daughter who can sing and copy music, and perhaps even look him straight in the eye and speak properly. That, however, still feels like a faraway dream, although as I put the small tails on the eighth notes, and graceful slurs over a group of sixteenths, I practise saying, "Hello, Papa, how was your journey?" and "Good afternoon, dear Papa, I trust your stay in Carlsbad was very pleasant," and all variations imaginable.

Mama comes down to supper looking pale. She smiles and assures everyone she's fine, and helps herself to carrots and potatoes and beef stew but doesn't eat any of it. "My stomach hurts a little," she says in response to Tante Lena. "Nothing that an early to bed and early to rise won't cure."

"Mama, should I call the doctor?" I ask, following her up the stairs after supper. "Remember what Herr Colm said about having to find one in Zerbst?"

She just laughs and touches her stomach lightly. "No. I'm going to have an early sleep and I'll be fine in the morning. It must have been something I ate yesterday. Can you make sure the boys are in bed in a half hour? Lise will help you—"

"Yes, Mama." I watch her walk, slightly bent over, to her room.

I have trouble sleeping. I try to hum the double concerto, looking up at the stars and the moon, to make me fall asleep, but it doesn't help. The moon looks like an onion with a small slice taken off. And the stars seem so far away. I light a candle and begin a letter:

July 3, 1720

Dear Girl,

What was wrong when I saw you in the mirror? Was it you that I saw there? It felt so cold. It gives me an ache ...

I can't write anymore, and blow out the candle and toss and turn, falling in and out of sleep. It's just becoming light—I can hear the birds trilling outside my window—when I tiptoe from my room, past Tante Lena's and the last flight of stairs to Mama's room. I smell vomit before I even open the door.

"Mama!" I rush in, and find her shivering on her side, huddled under the thick quilt although even so early the air is already hot. I can't see a trace of the vomit; she must have gone outside and disposed of it while everyone was sleeping. I feel her forehead. "Now you have a fever!"

"Oh, it's nothing," says Mama, trying to rise but falling back on the pillow.

"But it is something," I say. Her damp curls stick to her forehead. "Where does it hurt?"

"My stomach. Here," she points to the lower part. "I just need some breakfast."

"No! Wait right here! Don't move!" I run down the stairs to the room I share with Wilhelm. I shake him awake, and he looks at me as if I'm mad.

"Let me sleep!" He pulls the cover back and rolls away.

"No!" I shake him again. "Mama's sick. You have to help me make a sickbed for her in the sitting room by the kitchen. We're going to move the lounge bed from Tante Lena's sitting room."

"But—"

"Never mind. There isn't time." There must be something about my tone of voice because he follows me down the stairs and helps me set up the bed without a word, not one little whine.

"Now, to Mama's room. We'll help her move."

At first she protests and says she's fine, but after

a while she drapes her arms around both of us and we move slowly down the stairs. Tante Lena opens the door when we pass her room.

"What's all the fuss about, so early—" Then she sees Mama and turns pale. "Oh, my heavens. For the first time in her life, my sister is sick."

"I'm sure it's just a little fever," says Mama. I can feel her sweat through her nightdress.

"I must lie down. I think I'm going to faint." Tante Lena retreats back into her room.

After we have Mama settled, I order Wilhelm to fetch more well water for cold cloths to apply to Mama's forehead, and I wake and help to dress the younger boys, and prepare breakfast, and order that we have morning prayers as usual, by Mama's sickbed so that she can sing along, her head propped up on pillows.

"Oh, heavenly Father, I pray that ..." I sing out as I have never done, and look at Mama and sing with all my heart that she will be well soon. Tante Lena must still be in her room. I suspect she will not be much help in this ordeal.

Mama insists that Wilhelm still go to school, and before I send him off alone, I tell him to find Herr Colm at the palace. "He'll know where to find the doctor in Zerbst. He was just there. Ask him to go again and fetch that doctor. It's our only hope, since the court surgeon is with Papa and the prince."

Wilhelm nods solemnly, as if I'm head of the prince's army, and runs off. I head straight back to Mama's sick room to apply more cold cloths to her fever. I notice as I dip the cloth in the water that my hands are trembling. If only Lise would come—but it's her day off. If only Papa would come, or Herr Colm, or the doctor, or Tante Lena strong and able to make everything better again. Now I'm sorry for all the times I wished Papa wouldn't come home. Perhaps this is my punishment for being glad of his absence. Or perhaps it's my fault that Mama is so sick because of the maze, as Tante Lena seems to think.

Time crawls. I check Mama, and check on the boys, and sweep the hearth, and look out the window for Herr Colm, and check Mama again. It's late afternoon before I finally see the little man step out from his carriage. He's accompanied by a page carrying an armload of music.

"I was going to make a last visit, anyway, to drop off this music," says Herr Colm, when I fly down to the door. "You must inform your papa when he returns that I'm very sorry but have decided to resign as court copyist and move to

Berlin, where the pay is much better and the work less strenuous. You must tell him I'm very sorry to leave all this music unfinished, most particularly the Concerto for Two Violins, which is to be premiered the day after the prince's return from Carlsbad." He gestures wildly to the box the page is carrying right past me up the stairs, but I hardly notice it.

"Yes, yes, Herr Colm, but the doctor, did Wilhelm ask you about the doctor for Mama? She's sick."

He nods. "I'm on my way now. Zerbst is exactly on my route to Berlin. I'm sure Herr Dr. Eike will agree to travel here. He's a kind man, an expert in his field. He'll know what's wrong with your mama. But it may be tomorrow or the next before he can arrive, although I'll tell him to do his utmost to make great speed." He turns to the door.

"Herr Colm!" I'm desperate for him not to leave. "Can you send a messenger to Papa about Mama's sickness?"

He shakes his head. "Your papa is soon to begin the long return journey. You know as well as I that even the speediest mail coach would not intercept the royal entourage in time. Besides," he says, his face brightening, "your mama will be mended and healthy by that time, I'm sure. Why, just the other night I observed her in the highest spirits, laughing with you on the grass by the maze!"

Tomorrow or the next! I watch Herr Colm's carriage turn off the street and clench my fists to keep them from trembling. What am I to do?

The younger boys are crying by Mama's bed. "This won't do at all," I say, putting my arms around them and taking Johann on my lap. "We must do something to make Mama sleep." I look over at her and she manages a smile. "Let's sing her our favourite songs." In my new strong voice I sing with them, "Three Ships" and "Child's Prayer" and "Cakes and Cats and Baker." I prepare a broth for supper and feed a bit of it to Mama, and have Wilhelm take a tray to Tante Lena, who is now also ill, and as the sky turns dusky pink and purple, I stay by Mama's side and lose track of the number of times I cover her up and take off the covers and apply the cold cloths according to her chills and fevers.

"Thank you, Catharina, you should go to bed now," says Mama, after all the others have gone and I'm sitting by her side changing the cloths.

"I won't leave your side until you're better."

She laughs and then winces in pain. Now any movement makes her stomach hurt, and she has to lie very still. She doesn't sleep. The night is hot. I have the window open, but it doesn't help in the least. I've lost track of the times I've gone to the street to empty the bucket of vomit.

"Mama," I say after a distant clock strikes the hour of three. "Would it help if I sang and rubbed your stomach in the sore spot, in rhythm to the song?"

"Try," she whispers, and I begin to sing a hymn, "Now Thank We All Our God," but as soon as I touch the spot, she screams out in pain.

"I'm sorry, Mama," I say, and I'm sorry for so many things—that she isn't better yet, that Papa isn't home, that the doctor isn't here. I fall asleep on the hard floor and dream of the moonlit maze and Mama laughing and running again, and wake to half-light and the birds chirping a new day. I look to Mama, hoping my dream's come true and she's better. After all, she really has only been ill for one day, two if you count the day she didn't eat and stayed in her room. She's sleeping, finally. But her forehead is hot and she's as pale as the moonlight she ran through, laughing, in my dreams.

It's been two weeks since Dad made the maze, and we've run through it almost every day after supper. I still haven't figured out a way to ask him for Mom's violin. We're "deep into March," as Dad would say, but the weather's still cold as February, and there have been a few more blizzards, so we've even built up the walls of the maze and added some dead ends. The way it stays cold, we'll still be running it in May. Today at the end of it he announces that it's time for a father-daughter violin practice. "Do we have to?" I groan, wiping off my glasses as we come in from the cold.

"Once a month. You promised."

I always practised violin with Mom, right up until the time she went to the hospital. After she died, Dad and I agreed to keep up the tradition of parent involvement in my music. A good idea in theory, but the truth is it's a real pain. Dad turns into a professor and gets critical, but I don't take anything he says seriously because I know a lot more about playing the violin than he does, and even though he says he's just offering "objective positive feedback" or something like that, he gets very picky and it always ends in tears or me stomping off to my room and threatening to quit.

I don't expect anything different tonight as I lug my violin down the stairs and open my case. Dad is sitting in the large armchair by the grandfather clock in professor mode with bifocal glasses, his legs crossed, notebook and pen ready.

"On Saturday, if the weather finally gives us a chance, we can take the bus into the city and look for a full-size violin," he says, pushing up his glasses. "So even if it's just a trial, you can play on it for the assembly, which is … next week?"

"Next Tuesday. One week from today." Great start. Why did he have to remind me how soon the assembly is? I tighten my bow and sweep the rosin back and forth hard over the horsehair more times than I need to. "But that gives me only two days to get used to the new violin before the assembly. I need more time. I'll just have to play this old one." I lift it to my chin and accidentally bang the scroll on the music stand.

"Ouch!" says Dad. "I know you've outgrown this one, but you should always treat your violin as you would a baby. You have to show me that you're ready for a full size."

Doesn't he know that Mom always said the part about the baby? How can he just talk as if he's her?

She should be here—not here in this ramshackle old haunted house with its bats and creaks but in our house in Toronto, in her studio. *What should we start with today? How about a little review—"Minuet 3" by Bach—ready?* And we'd be off.

"I suppose we should start with the Bach Double since that's what you're playing in the assembly. Or perhaps the G major scale?"

I hate it when he tries to act as if he's Mr. Dekker or Mom or somebody. I ignore him and tune my violin.

"Hannah? What will it be? I don't have all night." His voice sounds edgy. I want to ask him what he has to do so urgently. The Door? The Floor? Maybe he'll be late for going to the store with the sled? "By the way, I can't remember, did you arrange everything for the rehearsal next week?"

"Yes."

"So is Bridget coming all the way out here the day before or—"

"Yes. Bridge the Perfect is missing her precious ballet to come out here after my lesson on Monday. They could've just come on Tuesday morning before school. But her mom insisted. She's one of those 'everything has to be perfect' types. Well, what else would you expect with a daughter like Bridget?"

"Hannah—"

I start to play the Bach Double before he can say anything else. I'm playing out of tune. And I'm scared I'm going to get lost. I haven't been lost in this since before that lesson when I heard Mom's violin so clearly. It was probably all in my stupid imagination—dumb, dumb, dumb—I'm never going to be able to play this piece, and where am I going? Somehow I make it to the end, but I have to speed up to get there because if I go at a steady tempo I know I'll get lost.

"Well," says Dad when I'm finally finished. "Well." He pushes up his glasses and sits back, and the tick-tock of the grandfather clock sounds between us like a time bomb about to explode. I strum my violin and look straight at the black of the music stand and wait. "Well. You made it through without getting lost."

He's trying to be like Mom, starting with something positive. I keep strumming.

"Hannah, you could at least look at me when I'm speaking. Honestly, you're not exactly acting like a twelve-year-old ready for a full size."

I turn and glare at him. I have to push up my glasses, which I hate, because it makes me look like him. Mom had perfect eyesight.

"Well," he continues, trying to act as if there isn't anything wrong. "Have you tried it slowly to make sure each note is in tune? The beginning, especially, didn't sound very—"

"How am I supposed to get it in tune if my fingerboard's way too small? My fingers are too big, and every time I play a note it's practically a semi-tone off. I need a full size."

"Hannah." Now he's using his exaggerated-patient voice, as if I'm one of his slower students. "You'll just have to be patient and wait until Saturday when we can—"

"If we had a CAR like every other normal person on this planet, we'd have been able to go to the city a long time ago—"

"Hannah." Uh-oh. Death-trap voice. Quiet and calm on the surface but actually about to explode. "Certainly not every person on this planet owns a car. In Africa alone, 77 percent ..."

He lectures on and on about statistics and pollution and the ozone. He just doesn't get it. Good old Dad, pulling his old wagon or sled, depending on the season, to Clear Lake Super Value Foods for milk. Doesn't he know that he's the laughingstock of town?

"You're not listening to me."

"Well," I say, trying to make my voice calm and polite although I want to scream. "You're not listening to me. You asked me to play in tune, but I can't unless I have a full-size." I pause, considering my next move. "Do you think … do you think …" Dad's face goes tight and white but I carry on anyway. "Do you think I could try her violin?" I'm careful not to say "Mom." "Just try it out and see if—"

"No." Wrong move. Now there's just silence, the way it was after the funeral when I got out her violin to try it out and Dad wouldn't speak for a week.

"Then I don't see how I'm supposed to play!" I yell, and slam my violin down into its case. My bow slips from my hand and lands on the cement part of the floor that Dad hasn't covered yet. The wood at the tip splits, a tiny crack.

"Hannah, you're quite out of control." He makes a move to pick up my bow.

"I don't care!" I scream, and stamp my foot dangerously close to the fallen bow. "What good is Mom's violin doing in your room? Just getting dusty, when I could be playing it. You're just … you're just the most selfish person on the planet and I wish we'd never moved to this stupid place and …

and ... I HATE you!" I run from the room and grab my jacket and shove on my boots and run out the back door, slamming it shut with all my strength. I run out to the maze and start kicking the walls. I kick and kick and hit them with my fists until they fall into ruins, just a bunch of crumbled chunks of snow.

I start to kick the next part and then collapse onto the snow. I lie on my back and look up at the stars. *Why did you have to go and leave? It's not as if you're really gone, either—I keep hearing your voice, things you said, the sound of your violin. That's almost worse than if you'd just disappeared. You were supposed to teach me the Bach Double. You said we'd play it together someday ...*

If Mom hadn't died. If I could play the stupid violin the way I want to. If I could have Mom's violin. If, if, if. I decide to go inside when my bum starts turning numb. I creep around to the front, hoping he's already up in his room reading, but when I sneak onto the porch and peek into the living room window I see him sitting exactly where I left him, only he's slumped over with his head in his hands. I turn around and go in the back door, and quietly as I can slip off my boots and jacket. I stop at the entrance to the living room before going up the stairs. I should go in and tell him I'm sorry. But … I can't. I climb up the stairs, trying not to creak, get into my room, and shut the door.

On my bed is the case, open, with my violin in it. At the tip of the bow, right over the fine line of the crack, is a thin piece of duct tape, holding it together for now.

Ten

Hannah

"AND WHERE DID YOU SAY you studied? At the Toronto Conservatory? You must have had such good instruction. I keep telling Donald, one of these days we're going to have to move out of this place and start thinking about Bridget's career. Right, Bridget? You know, you hear stories about these kids at eight years old—eight!—moving out to places like Philadelphia to study, well, I ..."

I stare out at the white fields. Bridget's mom, Mrs. Fensteen, sort of asks questions and then keeps on going without you having to say anything, so I'm safe just sitting here in the back staring out the window. I'm carsick. Any moment I could ask her to pull over and I'd have to run out and throw up in the ditch. Or maybe she won't be able to pull over in time and I'll have to open the window and do it over the side of their spotless grey car. "It's a *Porsche*," said

Bridget after I'd said sorry for knocking—actually, just touching—my case a little against the side as we were getting in. "It's Mom's car, but Dad cleans it every third day." Then she got a tissue from the front and wiped the spot where my case touched.

The thing is, I never get carsick. I read to Dad and Uncle Ted all the way from Toronto and didn't feel a thing. The assembly tomorrow—that's why I feel as if I'm about to crash. What if my bow shakes so hard that I can't make a sound at all? Or the sound comes out awful and scratchy and thin? What if I blank out completely right in the middle? And have to stop and hunt around for my book, with Melissa giggling in the back? Or worse, throw up right on the stage? "Gross!" they'll say and run off holding their noses.

It doesn't help that Mr. Griggs made a big deal of announcing it over the loudspeaker today, and Melissa and Brianne and Tracy came up to me and wished me good luck, then walked away giggling with Jeremy and Ben. "I can hardly wait," I overheard Tracy say. "Mr. Quack is playing piano. Introducing … Banana and Quack! It's the circus …"

I'm still on my old violin. Dad and I never made it to the city to try any full sizes on Saturday. Ever since the blowup last week, we haven't been saying much of anything. He's in his own world, working on the living room floor. The maze in the backyard is still in ruins. Saturday came and went without anyone mentioning violins, so I figured he thought I didn't deserve it, the way I'd acted. I didn't dare bring it up. So I'm stuck with the old one, even the duct-taped bow, which Mrs. Fensteen saw and said, "I've always made sure Bridget has at least two bows because you never know what can happen."

Bridget and I just played it through a few times at my lesson, and I made it through okay, although Mr. Dekker must have known I wasn't playing the way I can, because when I was packing up my violin he came over and patted my shoulder and said, "It'll be fine. Remember to breathe. And stick your hands under your armpits to warm them up before you go on. Most important, focus on each phrase, one at a time. She talks. You talk. It's a conversation. Back and forth. That's all there is. Don't even think about getting lost and it won't happen." He's even going to try to rearrange a rehearsal so he can make it out to Clear Lake to hear us.

"Hannah?" Bridget's turned around and staring at me as if I'm from Planet Loser. Sometimes I think I really am from there. Especially now if I have to ask them to stop. They're both wearing different kinds of perfume that mix together and drift to me in the back. "My mom asked you which exit into town she should take. Are you okay?"

"Um … I'm fine … um … you'll have to take the next one—we just missed the one by the graveyard. Sorry." Great. Now we're going to have to parade right down Main Street in this Porsche with me about to barf. Past all the billboards, over the tracks, and by the old grain elevator … just a few people still out shopping. It's almost dark. I try to breathe. Then I spot them—the whole gang—coming out of the drugstore. Melissa's kind of leaning on Jeremy, with Tracy and Brianne following like ladies-in-waiting. I try to duck, but it's too late—Melissa sees me and tells everyone and stares and gives a tiny queen wave. I sort of nod and slump down in the seat.

I rush out as soon as we pull into the school parking lot and run over to a snowbank. Nothing. If only I could just throw up all this worry, leave it in the snowbank and breeze into the school tomorrow as cool as a famous violinist like Hilary Hahn and just knock them speechless and everyone would love me and Dad would be proud and—

"Hannah?" Bridget and her mom are standing by the car.

I walk over. "I'm sorry. I get a little carsick sometimes."

"Goodness, why didn't you say anything? I could have made Bridget sit in the back and you could have been up with me. Next time, say something."

There's not going to be a next time, Mrs. Perfect. Not if I can help it. "Sorry," I say and we head into the school.

The gym is huge and empty, except for Mr. Franckowiak, who looks so small up on the stage at the piano. His music isn't small, though. He's warming up with some big crashing concerto, which he stops as soon as Mrs. Fensteen coughs.

She marches right up the steps as if she's the principal. "We don't exactly have a lot of time," she says, reaching right over Mr. F. and giving us an A to tune up, as if he couldn't do it. "We've come a long way for this, we have to make another trip out here tomorrow, and Bridget needs her sleep before a performance, even if it is just a school gym in a little town. I always say every performance counts, don't you think?"

Mr. F. nods. "I'm Jack Franckowiak," he says, extending his hand.

She takes it lightly, as if it's contaminated. "Gloria Fensteen. I understand you're the … the … uh … *caretaker*?"

He nods.

"Right." She turns abruptly away. "Girls? Are you ready? Why don't you stand over *there*, Bridget. Then the audience will have a chance of hearing you better. You *are* the first violin."

"Mom, they're equal." It's the first I've really heard Bridget say anything to her mom since we got in the car.

"What do you mean, dear?" Mrs. Fensteen clicks her high heels across the floor.

"The first and second violins. It's a concerto for *two* violins. We're equal. Mr. Dekker says, 'Two voices intertwined, two soloists.'"

Thank you, Bridget. I look over to give her a smile but she's concentrating on her fingers, moving them up and down the fingerboard to warm up.

"Whatever, dear. Now, I'll stand right here toward the back and see how things are for balance. Ready?"

She's planning on running the whole show, and she doesn't know a thing about it, just like Dad. Mom used to run my rehearsals. She should be here, sitting calmly in a chair with a notepad and the music. Or better—she should be standing where Bridget is with her violin under her chin. *We'll play it together someday.* Shut up, Mom, just shut up. You're not here, so why do you keep saying that?

Mrs. Fensteen is making some big motion with her arms. This gym is so huge. Tomorrow, all the little kids will file in first and sit in the front—

"Hannah!" Bridget whisper-hisses over at me. "Can you just start already? My mom's going crazy."

I nod at Mr. Franckowiak and he gives me a wink and we're off. I'm unsteady, shaky, I don't even know if I can make it to the solo at Letter A. All the little kids will file in and sit right in front of me, and then more kids will file in, and more and more. My tone is shaking, I'm playing out of tune. Bridget glares over at me. When the gym is all filled with kids, the Grade 6 class will file in, and very last of the whole class will be Melissa. She and the gang will lean against the back wall because there's no room to sit, and she'll fold her arms and smile up at me, her braces flashing—

My bow skitters to a stop. I don't know where I am—tangled up somewhere at the bottom of the first page.

"Hannah, I can't hear you," says Mrs. Fensteen, clicking up to the front.

"That's because she's not playing," says Bridget dully, tucking her violin under her arm impatiently. "What's up?"

I can't say anything. It's like those dreams where

you try to open your mouth to scream but nothing comes out.

"Well, well, let's just start again from the beginning, shall we?" says Mrs. Fensteen with a forced smile, glancing at her watch.

Mr. Franckowiak gives me a real smile. *Play the way I know you can play,* it seems to say, the kind of thing Mom would say, and I nod and start again. I'm playing the rhythm and notes, although they're out of tune and shaky, but it's all wooden, as if everything real has been drained out of it, and my arm gets all shaky and I don't even make it to A before I get lost again.

Bridget keeps on playing for a while, her beautiful tone echoing in the gym. Then she stops and gives a big sigh. "Why don't you just get your music? Even if you have to play with it, it would be better than this." She's right. I run down the stage steps to get my music from my case on the floor near the wall.

But instead of getting my music I'm loosening my bow. Taking off my shoulder pad. Snapping my case shut.

"What do you think you're doing?" says Mrs. Fensteen, her hands on her hips.

"I'm sorry," I say in this small voice that I can hardly hear. "I'm sorry you had to come all the way out from the city for nothing. But you won't have to come tomorrow. I ... I just realized I can't do this. I can't ... play. I'm sorry—"

"Well, I never," begins Mrs. Fensteen, her face almost purple with rage. "Making us come all the way out here, Bridget's precious time, her missed ballet class—"

"You could have at least warned us," snaps Bridget.

"Leave her be," says Mr. Franckowiak, and I only catch these words from out in the hall, because I'm running, running as fast as I can, down the empty hallway, grabbing my boots from the boot rack, shoving them on without lacing them, running out into the freezing cold air, down the middle of the dark, empty street, down the block, then another, the insides of my thighs rubbing against each other, but I can't feel a thing. Numb nose, numb toes, I have no scarf and my violin case clanks against my leg with each step.

I run around the back of the house and close the inside door as quietly as I can. Good. Dad is sanding the living room floor, and the machine is loud as a screaming cat. I place my violin carefully on the kitchen table in full view, get out a sheet of scrap paper and a broken dark green pencil crayon, and write "I QUIT" and place the sign on top of my violin case.

I find a few old scarves and wrap them around so that only my eyes show, put on some warm mitts, and lace my boots up this time. I run down the driveway and decide to head across the park. I don't know where I'm going. All I know is that I have to get away from that gym and Bridget and her mom and violin and music and Dad and the house and this town.

I head out of the park, past the curling rink and down the street past the post office, past the funeral home and the bowling alley and the old confectionery, across Railway Avenue. I run down the ditch and then I have to trudge over a bit of frozen marsh with deep snow to my thighs to reach the steep bank leading to the tracks. I try to climb up, but keep slipping and sliding, snow getting into my mitts and stinging my wrists, snow in my boots. My socks are sopping. I grab onto a bush and heave myself up.

The tracks. Step. Skip a tie. Step. That day in the hospital when I held her hand, I promised her I'd never quit. "You understand, don't you?" I say up to the stars, running down the tracks past the grain elevator. I look ahead. What if a train comes? I'll hear it and see it in lots of time to jump off. "I'm …

I'm not good enough. I'm not like Bridget the Perfect or Hilary the Head Girl or … you. I get lost and scared and …" I think of the wooden tone, the gym, Melissa's braces … "And I always lose the music, just like I lost …"

Step. Skip a tie. Step. On the day of her funeral, I couldn't cry or sing any of the hymns. I sat on the hard pew and couldn't feel anything, sort of the way my thighs feel now when they rub as I walk. I know they're there, but they aren't at the same time. I stared up at the stained glass and listened to the Bach Double. "I lose the music just like I lost you, " I say as loud as I can to the stars.

I'll get out of town as far as I can go, and I'll hitchhike or something, and I'll find a way to earn money, and I'll never have to—

I hear it before I see it. The blast of the train coming at me full tilt, like someone crying at the top of her lungs. I'm frozen in place for a moment, then jump off the side and tumble down the bank. I can feel the ground shaking, there's a blast of sound and wind and speed and noise, and I hear her violin in it somewhere, in the rhythm over the tracks. "Mom, oh Mom," I say, curling up in the snow, shaking and sobbing inside the sound. "Why did you leave?" I scream into the blast.

After it's finally passed, I touch my cheeks and feel my tears, warm and freezing at the same time. The train's long gone, but this dry, brown grass is still waving from the blast. Kind of the way it was with Mom. She was here and then she was gone, but she left so many things still alive, like music and the sound of her violin and me. I can't stop shivering. I turn around and start running down the tracks after the train, back the way I came. I'm still quitting. Tomorrow I'll fake the flu, and the next day and the next. I'll hide out in our house, help Dad with the renovations and get the mail.

I reach into my pocket and feel our post office box key. With all my practising, I've forgotten. I'll stop by on the way home, pick up the mail for Dad.

Catharina

All through the day I jump up at the sound of carriages in the hope that one is the doctor. Surely Herr Colm was able to find him and tell him how sick Mama is. All day she's been getting steadily worse. In the morning when I brought some broth, she tried to tell me that she didn't want anything to eat, but the movement of talking makes her stomach hurt too much. Never before have I seen Mama's face crease so in pain, as when she tried to shake her head and say the single word "No." All through the day Lise and I took turns changing the cloths and sponging her face and neck. Now Lise gathers her things. She must go home to her own family.

"Catharina, we're hungry," says Carl, as Lise gently shuts the door behind her. The three boys stand in a line with wide eyes, staring at me. Now I'm not invisible to my brothers, now when I would give anything for them to look beyond me as if I don't exist and run to Mama and hug her skirts and hear her laugh.

"Wilhelm, there are cold potatoes on the shelf. Take them out along with some bread and cheese—" He looks at me blankly, as if I've just told him to run to Carlsbad and fetch Papa. "Wilhelm, on the cutting board—" Still blank stares. I sigh and leave Mama's side and go to the hearth to check the fire and the hot water, then to the cupboard for plates and cups and food. One would think that Wilhelm, a Latin scholar, so adept at the clavier and composition, would be able to manage a few potatoes. But he must be in shock about Mama, poor boy. I decide this has to come to a stop.

"This evening we will have a short program, to

cheer Mama," I say, setting out the food and lighting the candles. The room glows in the fire and candlelight. Mama appears to be resting at last. Now, if only the doctor would come knocking on the door. "Wilhelm, you will play the clavichord. Carl and Johann, you will sing. Even Tante Lena will join in. I'm going to her room right now to fetch her, ill or not ill."

"But Catharina, what will *you* do, since you can't play the clavier or sing?" asks Wilhelm. The rascal. He knows very well that I can sing, especially since Papa's been away. Talk of a program appears to have loosened his tongue.

"I'll do something too—never mind," I say, starting up the stairs with a tray for Tante Lena. The plate and cups tremble. Hands, if you could just stay calm and strong for a moment, you might find a way to make Mama better.

I burst into the room without knocking. "We're having a short program, to cheer Mama," I start in before she can say a word. "And I would kindly ask that you come down and participate. I have to say, Tante, that I really could use your help in caring for Mama and the boys. I think Mama is much sicker at this point than you are, and if you had an ounce of loyalty to this family that has provided for you for so many years, or to your dear sister who's never done anything but help you, you'd get up, get dressed, and join us immediately."

I have never given such a long speech to any grown-up, much less Tante Lena. Her mouth opens, but she is unable to speak. I flounce out of the room before she has a chance to find her tongue. I slam the door and stomp down the stairs. I'm tired of being quiet for her. I'm tired of treating her like the Princess Agnes. Each stomp is to erase the mean things she's said to me since I was a little girl.

We're almost through our cold potatoes (Carl complaining that he's still hungry and isn't there any hot roast beef?) when she makes her appearance.

"No need to stare," she says, glaring at the boys and avoiding my eyes. "I'm feeling somewhat better this evening." She sees Mama and picks up her pace to the bed and kneels. "Maria Barbara ..." Her voice quavers and is so much softer than I've ever heard it, as if all her snappish speeches have gone floating somewhere out into the night.

Mama's eyelids flutter open. "Lena," she manages to say, "you've come. And Mama, and Papa? Did they come too?" She takes Tante Lena's hand. It must be the fever. My grandmama and grandpapa died ages ago.

"Mama! You're awake!" shouts Carl, and runs to her bed with Johann close on his heels.

"Not so loud, Carl," I say, but it's no use. He's asking when she'll be well again to make a roast for supper instead of cold potatoes.

Mama laughs and winces. "Soon ..." she says and tries to sit up but immediately collapses back on the pillow.

"Mama," I say, rushing over and helping Tante Lena to raise her pillow against the wall so that she can see us a little. We have to do it ever so slowly because every small movement makes her stomach hurt. "We're having an evening program for you, just like the kind they have for the prince, only here in our sitting room." I clear my throat and try to sound official, like the man who announces Papa's concerts at the palace. "We'll begin the evening with ... Wilhelm Friedemann Bach at the clavichord."

Everyone claps as he runs to the clavichord and bows. He plays a slow sarabande that reminds me of that day we spent by the river, its slow current and Mama's deep breathing beside me, the moist earth in my hands. I look over at Mama and see tears running down her cheeks, and with a pang I realize how empty the house has been without Papa playing his music. *Please, Papa, please come home soon, please ...*

I decide to perform after Wilhelm, or I'll lose my nerve. I've decided to sing "Today Is a Good Day," even though it certainly isn't, but maybe it will cheer Mama. I've had it memorized for weeks, have been singing it during chores, and have also been using it for copying practice. I stand before them, looking at the floor, and hear Madame Monjou's words ... *think about your voice coming from a deep place, from the bottom of your feet ... stand tall ... your voice is your instrument.* I lift my face, square my shoulders, and look straight at Wilhelm, then Tante Lena, and open my mouth to sing. My voice is shaky at first, but by the time I toss off the trills, Wilhelm's eyes are so wide that it's all I can do to keep from laughing.

"How did you do that?" sputters Wilhelm.

"Catharina has a fine voice. She'll—" Mama falls back on her pillow.

"Shh, Mama, you musn't try to speak." I rush to her side and stay holding her hand while Carl and Johann sing "Cakes and Cats and Baker" with actions, William accompanying with all kinds of flourishes and grace notes. Soon Carl is the baker chasing after Johann the cat, who runs giggling around the clavichord with the stolen raisin cake.

Even Tante Lena laughs. Mama doesn't laugh,

although I know she wants to but it would hurt her stomach too much.

Tante Lena clears her throat. "Thank you all for your performances. I can see plainly that your mother is cheered. Catharina's singing voice is indeed a surprise. Why, give it a few years and she'll rival Madame Monjou!" She glances at me and nods. Tante Lena has never thanked me before for anything, or given me one scrap of praise. "I, too, have a contribution, although a short one. It's a story about the day your mother was born." We all get settled more comfortably, and I notice the twitch of a smile on Mama's face.

"Although your grandpapa was a very serious and busy man, with many responsibilities as church organist and composer, your grandmama, who also was named Catharina, by the way, was the opposite! Ah, she was a great teller of jokes and inventor of practical ones! Remember the herring in the organ loft, Maria?"

Mama smiles and nods.

"Tell it! We've never heard it!" says Wilhelm, but Tante Lena shakes her head. "Another time. This time ... she was of course great with your mother about to be born, and was at supper, and telling the story of your uncle Johann Christoph sleeping and snoring up in the organ loft. Then she began to laugh. Never in all my twenty years to that day had I seen her laughing as she did that night. Well, soon it was no laughing matter because your mother was kicking to be born. The midwife was called, and all night your grandmama Catharina groaned in the pangs of childbirth, but just as dawn came, to the ears of us waiting anxiously in the kitchen, there were peals of laughter, then the cry of a baby, and the midwife came out with your mother in her arms. 'What was all that laughter about?' asked your grandpapa, serious as ever and taking your mother in his arms. 'Oh,' said the midwife, 'your wife in the last minute decided to tell me about snoring Uncle Johann and so little Maria Barbara came into this world in the midst of our laughter!'

"Never had I seen such a look of surprise on your good grandpapa's face!" says Tante Lena, shaking her head and chuckling. We all laugh too, and in the midst of it I hear such a laugh. It's Mama, and it's the laugh of the moonlit maze and the sunlit kitchen and the picnic by the stream. I quickly turn to her. Could she be getting better? I watch her face, which suddenly twists in pain as her laughter turns into a high and loud scream. Her hands jerk to her stomach, and then away.

"Mama!" the boys shout, moving in closer, but Tante Lena guides them, protesting, toward the stairs to their rooms. "Enough for one night," she says. "Catharina, I'll take care of the boys. You tend to your mother."

Mama is lying back, trembling, her face so white, with small beads of sweat breaking all over her forehead and neck and running in small streams down her skin. I apply the cold cloths. I whisper, "Mama, you must rest now, and when you're well we'll hear more about Grandmama, and we'll laugh as loud and long as we want, the way we did on the grass outside the maze."

"Catharina—"

"Mama, you musn't speak—"

"The girl," she says in such a small voice that I can hardly catch her words, "the girl who isn't afraid ..."

"Yes, Mama—"

"After the maze ... I ..." Every word is an effort.

"Mama, please—"

"... I believe in her. I believe in you. So strong ... memorizing ... Latin ... singing ..." She turns her head and then winces at the movement.

"Rest, Mama," I say, applying the cloths. She breathes in short puffs, rapidly.

Three short knocks. The doctor! The blessed doctor! I leave Mama's side and fly through the kitchen, down the narrow stairwell to the door. I open it, and he takes off his hat and bows a little. "I am Dr. Eike," he says, rosy-cheeked and calm. "I have come to see the wife of the famous *capellmeister* Bach. You must be the daughter. Come, show me to your mama and tell me about her."

I lead him up the stairs and tell him everything that's happened since her not wanting to eat on the day after the maze. With each word, I feel a heaviness lift. He sets his bag—so filled with medicines and cures!—on the table beside Mama's bed and feels her wrist and neck for a pulse.

"She laughed just before you came," I say, wishing he would just open his bag and give her something. "It was a healthy laugh, like from before she became ill. I thought it meant she was getting better but then she screamed."

He nods. "It hurts her always here?" He motions to her stomach.

I nod.

He opens his bag and takes out a bottle. "You are to be congratulated for all you have done to support and comfort her. There is nothing more I could have done had I arrived earlier. This medicine is only for the pain, to make it a little easier. Your mother has perityphlitis, a common enough ..."

I don't understand a word he's saying. I'm just looking at the bottle in his hands, at the dark liquid that will make Mama better.

"... and you need some fresh air and sleep, a young girl such as yourself, at your mama's sickbed for so long. I know it is late, but will you find the pastor and bring him here? Then on your return you must get some sleep."

Why should I find the pastor? He only lives across the corner in the parish house, but I told Mama I wouldn't leave her side until she was better.

"Go on, the fresh air will do you good. Don't worry, I'll take care of your mama."

I nod and find my shawl. Tante Lena creaks down the stairs. "The doctor is here!" I tell her. "He has medicine for Mama!"

"And where are you off to?" she asks.

"Oh, the doctor sent me to get Pastor Berger. I'd much rather stay with Mama, but he said he'd take care of her—"

"Well then, hurry," she says sharply, in the voice of the Tante Lena I know, not the one who laughed and told the story just an hour ago. She rushes to Mama.

I lift my long skirts and run down the empty street to the corner. Was that a pack of rats scurrying out of my way? What are those shadows looming by the hedge? There is the yowl of a cat, and somewhere a yipping dog. I want to run away, but something makes me stand for a while before the parish house gate. What use can the pastor be? Perhaps he will read words of comfort, to help along with the medicine. I finally walk to the door and lift the heavy knocker.

I'm afraid he will come down in his nightshirt, but he's dressed as if to go out, cape already in hand. I tell him of my errand, and before I can catch my breath he's fetched a wooden box and we're out the door and hurrying back.

Tante Lena and the doctor sit by Mama's side. I fix my eyes on Pastor Berger as he opens the box and pulls out a silver communion goblet and a small flask of wine. The sacrament! But why here in our sitting room? This is for church on Sunday mornings, when we line up to receive the wafer and the wine. Besides, Mama can't take any food, even if it is Christ's Holy Body and Blood. I've tried all day and she just heaves it up.

Sure enough, she gags on the wafer and the tiniest bit of wine. "Our dear Father in Heaven …" Pastor

Berger begins to pray and I look out the window at the waning moon, a bit like the communion wafer with a bite taken out, and say my own prayers. I thank God that Dr. Eike is here at last and has brought the medicine.

"There is nothing more we can do," says the doctor after the prayer. He nods to Pastor Berger, who packs up his box and turns to leave, and to Tante Lena, who looks at me as if she means to say something, then turns away and slowly walks to her room.

"You must sleep," says Dr. Eike, patting me on the shoulder and gently steering me from the room. "You've been a very brave girl, all these days taking care of the household and your mama."

I shake my head and turn back to Mama's bed. "Did she talk while I was gone? Is the medicine working?"

The doctor slowly shakes his head. "As I said, the medicine was only for pain. There was nothing I could do that you could not have done. She's in a state between life and death. She is breathing, but would not waken now even if you shook her very hard and shouted in her ear. It's always this way with perityphlitis, the course of the illness—"

He rambles on in a language I don't understand. All I heard was the word *death*. I kneel by Mama's side and take her wrist. There is a heartbeat, so fast, like the allegro from one of Papa's concertos. "No!" I interrupt. "She has a pulse. She's breathing. I won't leave her side until she's well again."

"As you wish," says the doctor gently, and sinks into the armchair by the clavichord.

The Concerto for Two Violins—this is what I will hum, in rhythm to Mama's pulse, until she opens her eyes and laughs again. It's the music of God—Papa himself said he wrote it to glorify God—and it had the power to lead me out of the maze. I stroke Mama's wrist and feel the beat and hum with all my might, until I see Dr. Eike drowsing in his chair, until my knees are numb underneath me, until I have gone through the first and the second and the third movements uncountable times, until I'm sure Papa on his way from Carlsbad must surely hear my humming, and the girl, so far away, has heard me and is answering back.

The birds trill and the sun begins to rise just as I finish the second movement for what is probably the fiftieth time. When I take the pause before the beginning of the third movement, there is a flicker in Mama's wrist, and then a pause. And then I know I can't sing this music any longer, because the beat has stopped. I stand up and squint at the sun. Soon,

I will run to Pastor Berger's again. I will tell him to toll the great bells, and then all of this city will know that my mama is dead.

———

Wait. For the bells to toll. The afternoon heat soaks clothes to the skin, flies gather on neck, in hair. Here come Tante Lena and the boys. Slow. They leave the door open. On the landing is an oak coffin, covered with a black pall. Tante Lena takes your hand. Pull away. Don't touch her hands, pale and wrinkled that with your own hands washed the body yesterday. Cold forehead, cold cheek ...

Wait. There are the bells. Sound of lead, cold down to the toes. Here come the people of town, Frau Fischer, Herr Friedel, the schoolchildren, the man with the pipe, even old, mad Salome from down the lane. Here come the carriages, a cluster of Bachs, like flies in black satin, moving in. More carriages, fancy with gold at the windows. From the palace. Pages, ladies-in-waiting, Herr Felici, even Her Highness Mother the Princess Agnes.

Sweat down the back. Here comes Pastor Berger in a white cassock. And sexton and pallbearers in black. And here ... here come the Latin school teachers—rector, conrector, cantor, the whole choir of boys. Yesterday you opened the doors of their school. You stood tall. Before they could even open their mouths to sing "Clumsy Catharina" you told them, finally, you shouted at them to keep quiet. You swept past them, shocked from the sound of your voice, and opened the door to the rector's office, asked for the choir. "Of course," he said, shaking your hand as if you were a man. "The full choir will sing. And, out of respect to your great father, we will greatly reduce the cost. Only ten groschen instead of a thaler for me, less for the others, mere pfennig." You must remember to pay him after it is over, with coins from her room in a bag at your waist.

Wilhelm joins the choir at the front of the procession. The pallbearers lift the coffin and carry it to the front. Slow. All the men make a line behind the choir. Now you. You. Tante Lena pushes you out behind the men. A thumping heart. Sweat. You are the eldest child of the dead. Step. Step. Lift your foot and place it down. You must lead all the women and girls. Don't trip. You are leading Her Royal Highness Princess Agnes down the street. Step. Step. Don't look back and up at the apartment window. She will not be there, waving goodbye.

Walk. The boys sing "Cease Now to Mourn," their clear voices winding through the crowd, down to the marketplace, mixing with the crying of the women behind. Don't stop. Slap a fly. The sun is hot. Thirst. You must keep walking, with your head up, for her.

Here is the green place where she will lie, by the weeping willow and the oaks. Past the gate, place your pfennig in the basin for the poor. Here is the hole, and the coffin to be set in it, the sexton with his shovel, the pastor with his Bible. Hymns. Why must we sing? So many hymns. "In Peace and Joy I Now Depart" and "If Favours We Receive from God." The way she sang. Her laugh after Tante Lena's story. The pulse in her wrist as you sang through the night.

Can't sing. Can't talk. Dry throat. No tears or notes for her. No tears, only the trickle of sweat. And flies. You should cry. You should sing. Not one note or tear. Even Tante Lena cries. "Commit your fortunes to the Lord, and He will sustain you ..." begins the pastor. He reads on and on. The willow rustles, as if it has ears and a voice. Its branches hang like arms. Rustle. Can it hear a wooden heart? The sexton shovels the dirt. Plop. Plop. In rhythm to the Latin of the choir. Slow. Plop. Another. Another. On and on. She is covered.

Another hymn. "In the Midst of Life We Are." Trees laughing! Laughing, the way she did in the

maze. Say goodbye to the trees. Say goodbye to …
to … turn around. Step. Step. Over the grass. Do
not look at the lilacs, so green without flower. Past
the basin of alms. You must keep your head up, lead
the women back through town.

Head up. Step. Step. Papa home in three days.

Eleven

Catharina

How many times have I rehearsed what I will say to him? How many times have I swept and dusted this landing? Each time I hear a carriage, I jump and run to the window, expecting to see Papa stepping out with all his instruments. Then the horses continue to clop down the street and I return to my dusting.

It's the only thing I can do. Oh, I've held Carl and Johann in my arms, tried to hush their crying and answer their questions. "Where is Mama now?" "In heaven, of course." "But what's she doing?" "Probably singing and copying music. And laughing, of course." "But why would she laugh when we're all crying?" And on and on until I want to yell at them to be quiet and I want to run away. Thank goodness they're both finally napping.

Wilhelm has been sulking and playing the clavichord every blessed waking moment. This morning I finally persuaded him to go to school. "Papa will be home today and what if he catches you sitting here spoiled and sulking? He would expect you in school like a proper Latin scholar. You must be brave, Wilhelm—"

"Very well." With a pout, he scooped up Lumpi and then dumped her hard on the floor so that she yowled and ran away.

"Wilhelm! What's Lumpi done to harm you?" I had trouble keeping the impatience out of my voice. "Now go and get dressed for school."

"I'm only doing it because of what you said about Papa, not because I'm obeying you. You didn't even cry for Mama," he said and stomped past me up the stairs.

"You'll be late," was all I could say because I wanted to have the last word and I hated my voice with that hard cold edge in it, like Tante Lena's. At the funeral, all kinds of Bach relatives offered kind words and food, but not one offered to stay and help. I suppose they assumed Tante Lena and Lise would do the job. That's all fine, except Tante's never out of her room except for mealtimes and then seems to find plenty of energy to tell Lise and me that we've underboiled the red cabbage and overboiled the potatoes and left the roast to burn. The night she told the story about Mama, when her voice warmed up and she made us all laugh, seems like an eon ago. Now I'm just like her, trying to boss Wilhelm. I can't even cry for Mama, not a single tear. What kind of a daughter is that?

I stand up from the table I'm dusting and look in the mirror. There's no other girl there, because of course that's all she was, just a silly imagining, a game. There's just me, Clumsy Catharina. The Concerto for Two Violins keeps trying to sneak its way into my head, but I won't allow it. How silly I was, to think some old music could actually save Mama. "Fool," I hiss into the mirror and make the ugliest face, gritting my teeth and shaking my fist at my reflection with such a force I shudder and have to turn away.

I plop down on the first step and shove my face into my arms. The lace of my cap scratches my cheek and so I whip it off and fling it a few stairs down.

"Hello! Maria Barbara! Hello!" I jump up at the sound of Papa's voice and take a few steps down. The door flings wide open and he stands in the entrance, a violin case in his hand. He's dusty from the long journey but is wearing the rosiest cheeks and the biggest smile, as if he's about to open the most precious gift in all of Europe. He looks so excited, like a young boy, like Wilhelm when he received the *Little Clavier Book*.

My heart begins to make a racket. My knees begin to shiver, the same as always when Papa stands before me. What will I tell him? All my rehearsed speeches fly away, even the one I wrote out and folded into my pocket. "Papa—"

"My dear girl!" He runs up some stairs and gives me a hug, looks past me to the top, to the door he thinks she'll open at any moment. "You aren't married yet, I see!" He laughs, a laugh full of the sun and music and forests he must have soaked up on his journey home. "But you've dropped your cap!" He picks it up and hands it to me, his eyes still fixed on the door above me. "Wherever are your mother and the boys and Lena? I expected them all down here at the first sound of my voice! Maria!" His voice echoes in the stairwell. "Are you playing a trick?" He laughs again and makes a move to pass.

I wish I could run out of this door and down the Stift Street and out of Cöthen. I'd find a ride on a wagon to Leipzig or Berlin and never have to tell Papa. He'd have to find out some other way. But there is no one else. My legs are roots. They won't let me move until I tell.

I take a few steps back and up so I'm again at the top of the stairs, blocking his path. I fold my arms across my chest and take a huge breath, although my knees are quaking as usual. But I'm finally taller than him. "Stand tall! He is no giant! See, you're looking down on him from above!" the girl's voice whispers, and my heart slows a little.

"This is most ridiculous!" booms Papa. His jovial smile begins to fade. "Are you and your mother playing a trick? Wherever is she?" He looks behind me again.

"Papa," I manage to say in a small voice and stare straight at him until he's forced to stare right back into my eyes. I've never noticed before how dark they are, and now, so much at the surface of them, like the sound of the violin rising to the top of all the instruments in one of his concertos. "I have something important to tell you. Please ... we must go somewhere else ... to your studio."

Have I really just proposed to my papa that we enter his own private studio for a meeting? I want to run away again, but then I think of the sound of the bells tolling, and slowly turn to open the door. "Come, Papa," I say. I think he's a bit shocked from my speech and manner, because he follows me without a word through the kitchen and up the stairs. Thank goodness the boys and Tante Lena are napping—otherwise they'd come racing out in tears and blurt it out and Papa would faint from the shock.

He sits at his desk, and I sit in one of the big hard chairs facing him. It's as if we're here for an important business conference, just Papa and me. I look down at my hands.

"Well? I demand you tell me immediately the meaning of all this. Where in heaven's name is your mother?"

I keep looking at my hands. These hands that washed her cheek after she died. "Papa," I say and feel all the tears that wouldn't come now welling up in my throat. I musn't cry. I swallow, breathe, look him straight in the eye. "She is now buried … almost three days."

His fist slams the desk. He scrapes his chair away and stands, his face white and then red, and he stomps to the window, his back to me. "Why … was I not informed?"

"A message never would have reached you in time. Her illness was so rapid. The doctor called it perityphlitis." There. It came out right, the word I've practised so many times. "She became slightly ill on July the third, more so the next day … and"—why do the tears want to come now, just when I want to be so clear and precise—"died early in the morning on the sixth day of July. She was buried on the seventh." I swallow again and again. How can I speak of it like this? As if I were the sexton or Pastor Berger.

With his back still to me, he fires off the questions rapidly, like staccato notes. Why did the doctor take so long? Where was Tante Lena? What happened when she first became ill? Who was there when she died? Did she take the sacrament? Were the great bells tolled? Was the full Latin choir employed? At what cost? How was this paid? Each question I answer as quickly and precisely as possible, swallowing all the while until I think I will burst with gulped tears.

"Enough," he almost whispers after every last detail has been asked and answered. Not once did I hesitate, or give a dubious answer, or let the swallowed tears break my voice. "Go now. And tell the others I will not be disturbed."

"But, Papa, the boys … Wilhelm and Carl will want to—"

"No." His voice is thin and empty. "No one will enter this room unless requested. Clear?" He still faces the window.

"Yes, Papa." I exit and run down the stairs to my room. I scoop Lumpi with me under the quilt. And then the tears come.

———

"But why won't Papa see us?" Wilhelm slams his fist down on the table in a manner that reminds me of Papa this afternoon. "We've been waiting for hours." Wilhelm is in an even sulkier state than when he went off to school. He doesn't wait for my answer and stomps off to the clavichord, begins with the first piece from the *Little Clavier Book*. I can tell he means to play through the whole book right to the end, as if his playing will entice Papa downstairs.

Papa hasn't come out since I left him up there hours ago. The coachman unpacked all his bags and instruments and kindly brought them upstairs, where they sit in a forlorn heap outside Papa's studio. Lumpi is especially fond of the violin case and has been sitting on top of it like a princess.

"He'll come out when he's ready," I assure the younger boys. "Hush, now, off to bed. I'll come up later and sing songs with you if you're ready and quiet." They move up the stairs, both of them crying and whining for Papa.

I begin to make up a supper tray for Papa. I know he ordered no entrance, but he must be famished. Why, he arrived back from Carlsbad shortly after the noon meal and has been up in his study ever since. And even though music feeds the soul it hardly cures a growling stomach. I set out our best dishes and pour wine into a goblet from the glass cupboard. I even run outside and snip a rose from the trellis in front of the house and place it in a vase. Now, if I can only avoid tripping on my way up the stairs, as well as Papa's rage at the sight of me. He will stand so tall behind his desk, with his red face and shake his fist at me and … I pause for a moment before the door. He must eat. I will tell him this. And that the boys need him.

He's behind the desk with his head buried in his arms, sobbing. I watch his shoulder heave again and again, his wig completely askew. *This is Papa.* From now on, whenever I hear his music, watch him lead the *capelle* with his wig perfectly in place, with all the notes and lines of his music in some heavenly order, I will not think of the great Johann Sebastian Bach but of Papa sobbing for Mama. He is not God on his throne, not a judge or a giant. In each sob there is a heart breaking like mine.

I tiptoe over, place the tray on a table by the desk. "Papa," I whisper, and find the nerve to touch him lightly on the shoulder. He raises his head and looks at me with swollen eyes. "Papa, you must eat. I've brought a tray. And the boys … need you." I turn to leave.

He touches my arm. "I am … sorry."

"Papa?" I turn back.

"For my earlier behaviour. All those questions. You must have been frightened to the heavens during her illness. You've had enough to deal with, never mind answering all your old papa's questions. You must understand my shock—"

"Yes, Papa. I understand." I touch his shoulder again. "She … she was my best friend, too. She … was … everything."

The tears slide down his face again. I see that they are smudging the music on his desk. "Papa, the music …" I pull the page away. The Concerto for Two Violins. This music must follow me.

"The premiere performance is tomorrow," he says. "The prince has said after the long journey he is hungry for more music. He said it's the music that keeps his health. I must finish copying these parts. Herr Colm—"

"He told me to tell you he has resigned as

copyist. He's now in Berlin. You know, he fetched Dr. Eike in Zerbst on his way."

"Ah," says Papa. "Then I must finish. I know the prince. Even when he hears of my loss, he won't postpone tomorrow's performance. He thinks first of himself, always." Papa's shoulders slump. His face is drawn and white, so tired.

"You must rest." I clear my throat and straighten my shoulders. "Papa ... I ... I will copy these for tomorrow's performance."

He raises his dark eyebrows.

"Wait here." I dash to my room and retrieve the neat stack of sheets, my best samples of work since the lessons with Mama. I run back into his studio and place them on his desk.

He studies them carefully, sheet after sheet. "This ... is exemplary work." His eyebrows are still raised. "She taught you?" His voice is slow and heavy.

I nod, and gently help him to his feet. "Now, Papa, really, you must rest. I'll copy this for you. It's not that much, because you've assigned only one instrument for each part. Just a small ensemble will play, no?"

Again he raises his eyebrows in surprise. "You know my music?"

Know it! "When she was"—I force myself to look at him and say the word—"dying ..." He closes his eyes. "I ... I sang and sang ... this ..."

I know I must sing the second movement for him. But what if I open my mouth and nothing comes out? Or worse, if it comes out horribly, Papa will think a squawk was the last sound Mama heard. *Truth.* What she really heard, when I took her hand and felt her fast pulse, was ...

I close my eyes and begin. The sound is thin at first, but I think of Mama, and the way her hand felt that night, how I thought the music could save her, and somehow the sound keeps coming out of me, stronger and stronger, as if, as Madame Monjou said, I'm a well, and my voice is coming from a deep, dark place big as the night sky filled with stars and an ache for Mama.

And then I hear the other part, on the violin, fitting in with my voice, our two melodies criss-crossing and winding around each other just as they did when I found my way out of the maze. I open my eyes and see Papa playing his new violin— his eyes still swollen from sobbing and his face still drawn and tired—but the sound coming from his bow over the strings clear and strong. I lose track of how long we play and sing together—we reach the end of the second movement and then begin it again, and sometimes I close my eyes and sometimes open them to see Papa's eyes closed, and once we both have our eyes open at the same time, and we look across the music at each other and I know we're both remembering Mama.

Finally, we reach a silence. Papa's bow comes to a stop, and suddenly I feel so exhausted that I want to fall in a heap on the floor and sleep for days and days. And I wonder where Wilhelm is, why he hasn't barged in yet demanding to be part of the music, too. Papa just stays silent, looking at me for a long time.

"Catharina," he says finally, gently putting down his violin. "I am sorry. I ... I have not been fair. For years ... I have not been fair. I haven't listened to you. Why, you've been singing right in front of me all this time in morning prayers and I haven't heard you at all. Such a voice. And all you did for her during her illness. I'm ... I'm very proud of my only daughter."

At Papa's words, something else washes around inside me along with all the sadness for Mama, and I realize this is the first time I've ever heard Papa say my name. I look down, because I'm not used to looking him straight in the eye for so long, and because my face is warm from his praise, and I see his new violin glinting from its case, glinting and calling for me to touch it again.

"Papa," I say with a bold edge in my voice I've never heard, "may I … hold … your new violin? Just for a moment?"

"My violin? Whatever for?" I see surprise harden his face, and I look down at the floor again, but in a moment he's reaching into his case and holding it out to me like a gift. "You must be careful not to touch too much of the varnish. Hold it with just your fingertips."

As soon as my skin touches the wood, I feel dizzy and close my eyes, and a vast space opens up all around me. In a great cathedral—bigger than the Jakobskirche or even the Thomaskirche in Leipzig—I see the girl again, sobbing as if her heart will break. It *is* the girl in the mirror of the maze gazebo and she *has* lost someone—someone she loved with all her heart. She has lost her mama. I want to tell her that music can't make Mama alive again, it won't take the ache away. But it gives you a place to put the ache—like throwing turnips into a pot of stew so you can stir it all around and feel the warm steam on your face for a while instead of the awful numbness.

"Let me in!" Wilhelm's voice, followed by a loud banging on the door. Papa and I look at each other. The girl is gone. I feel the wood under my fingertips one last time as I hand the violin back to Papa.

I open the door not only to Wilhelm but to Carl and Johann and even Tante Lena, who crowd in and rush over to Papa.

"How I've missed you all," says Papa, sitting down in the big armchair and taking Johann on his lap. There's a silence—a gap in the circle where Mama should be.

"Is Mama really in heaven laughing now?" asks Johann. "That's what Catharina told—"

"Good gracious! Laughing in heaven! What kind of ideas—" says Tante Lena.

"Papa, I've played all the way through your book," interrupts William, and then there's a general uproar around Papa for the longest time. When everyone's finally gone off to bed, and Papa has slowly climbed the stairs to his room, I rush to the place where Mama kept her copy supplies. I take the bag into Papa's studio and sit behind his big desk. I place the ink pot and rastrum carefully in front of me, then reach into the bag for Mama's favourite quill.

Hannah

I pull open the door to the post office, breathe in the musty smell of old paper and oil and something I can never figure out. The queen smiles from behind her glass frame. She looks so perfect with her gown and blue sash and crown. People like Bridget and Hilary the Head Girl become queen, not me. All I can do is pick up the mail. I put my key in Box 549 and don't even look through the window—behind it is just the dumb old place where they sort letters, of course, not some other magical time.

I grab a bunch of flyers from our box and lay them on the table that's messy with flyers people have left behind. About five obituary notices sit on the windowsill, and I swipe them off and throw them in the recycling bin. It makes me feel a tiny bit better. Of course there's no real mail. I toss all of it in recycling and glare up at the queen as if everything's her fault.

"When I was a girl, before she was queen, we used to sing a song, 'God Save the King,' about her father," says a voice behind me. Peppermint Woman. How did she get in so quietly? She starts humming a melody I remember from somewhere as she opens her mailbox. Her voice is thin and clear, comforting somehow, enclosing the two of us in this warm and lit-up place. I think of the tracks and shiver a little. She closes her mailbox and stops humming.

"Oh, don't stop—that was nice." I pull on my mitts.

"Why, thank you," she says, her face warming up with a hint of a smile. "I used to sing quite a lot when I was younger. Where's your violin?" She fishes around in her purse and pulls out a peppermint.

"It's … it's … I … how did you know about my violin?"

She sniffs. "You're always carrying it with you. And of course I can recognize a violin case. I'm quiet a regular concert-goer." She hands me the peppermint.

"Thanks," I say, pocketing it. "You might be interested to know there's a concert tomorrow at my school." Oops—that slipped out before I could stop it.

"What sort of a concert?"

"I … well …" What should I say? If I tell her about the assembly, then I'll have to play. And how can I play if I've decided to quit?

"Cat got your tongue? You usually seem to have enough to say for yourself."

"It's ... just an assembly thing tomorrow morning at school."

"And you're going to play the violin?" She actually looks interested.

"Well ... I'm supposed to play the Bach Double, but I'm not sure yet whether I'll play—" Dad will be frantic about me. "Um ... I have to get going. Bye." I make a beeline for the door.

"I love the Bach Double," she calls as I race down the steps to the street. There's a warm wind against my cheeks; by the time I reach the park, I've started to sweat.

Dad's standing at the window, and he runs down the driveway to meet me as soon as he sees me. "Hannah!" He gives me a huge hug. "Where on earth were you? I sent out Jack with his car to search and was about to call the RCMP. Where were you? I ... I was so worried I—"

"Dad! Oh, Dad, I'm so sorry." I pull him into the house. "I never should have raced off like that. It was dumb, I had a terrible practice and I knew I couldn't play, and I wrote this—" I point to the "I QUIT" sign on my violin that's still sitting in the middle of the kitchen table.

"Where on earth did you go?" Dad's racing around the kitchen trying to find the kettle for tea and some clean mugs. He comes back to the table and sits down and then jumps up again.

"Just walking along the tracks—"

"The TRACKS?" Dad's voice gets all squeaky, and he pushes up his glasses.

"It's okay." I get up and put on the kettle and put the tea bags into the pot. "I thought about a lot of stuff … about Mom …" I look over at him but he doesn't flinch. "And this train came—"

"A train?"

"It's okay. I jumped off the tracks. It went *by* me. I cried and cried. I never could cry at the funeral." I feel the peppermint in my pocket and start to feel a kind of calm. It's such a relief to talk about Mom with Dad.

"I couldn't either. Until tonight. Hannah … I … I'm sorry. I've been locking her up, as if that would keep her alive. It's … it's time we started talking about her, letting her out where she belongs." He goes into the living room and comes back with her case.

"Dad …"

He places the case on the table, opens it, and slowly takes her violin out of the satin bag. "I've been foolish and … selfish. This is yours. She meant for you to have it. Even if you never play again, you'll always have it." He places it in my hands.

Mom's violin. It's been three years since it's been played. I'm scared I'll drop it, my hands are shaking so much. "You know it's a very precious instrument," says Dad, staring at the violin as if it could vanish any moment. "It was made in 1720 by someone named Georg Aman." All I can do for a while is hold it on my lap. I stare down through the f-holes and at the bridge, then look up at the case and the blue draw-string bag. The envelope, the one that slipped out when I was in Dad's room that time …

Dad raises his eyebrows a bit as I reach forward. "In the bag," I say, "I think there was …" I hesitate with my hand in the air, but Dad just nods, so I go ahead and pull out the envelope. I tear it open, take out the tiny, folded paper, and read out loud:

"My daughter, not yet born,
*   You will be a girl, and you will play the*
violin. How do I know this? Because every day
I hold my violin under my chin and it speaks
to me, tells me where it has been and where it
will go. One day it will make music under your
fingers. And your sound will rise up under
your bow, a sound that is your own yet carry-
ing something of all the others who have played
it before you. Listen for us when you play …"

Tears are running into Dad's beard as I slowly lift the violin to my chin. It smells like Mom's lotion and varnish and something very old. The bow feels heavy. I've been waiting so long for this moment, and now that it's finally here, it's as if everything is moving in slow motion and I can't even get the bow to the string. Somehow I get it there and pull the bow back and forth over the A string, over and over, and close my eyes, and listen to the sound I haven't heard since she died. I close my eyes tighter. I can pretend she's still right here playing—I'm listening to her sound again, I'm lying in bed as she practises her scales …

I tune and start on a G major scale. Ouch. Out of tune on the shift. That's definitely me—Mom never would have been out of tune there. I realize with a shiver that I could stand here playing Mom's violin all night but it won't bring her back. What did I think—that somehow she'd genie out of her case if I could just get it open? I keep going up the scale and nail the high G at the top. *Bravo,* Mr. Dekker would say. I play the note again—it doesn't sound like Mom. It sounds like me.

The phone rings. I open my eyes to see Dad rushing to get it. "Sorry about not calling earlier. She got home and I was so happy I forgot about everything," says Dad. "The assembly? Well, I don't know, I guess I'll let her tell you." He hands over the phone.

"Hannah, you're safe," says Mr. F.

"Thanks for sticking up for me at the rehearsal. I heard you as I was running out." I clutch the letter from Mom. I want to say more but I don't know how.

"There *is* going to be a concert, yes?"

I look over at Dad's wet face and think about the gym full of kids and how cold my hands get when I'm nervous, and think about how Mom used to hug me after a performance. But mostly I think about how the violin just felt under my chin, the strings under my fingers. I look again at the letter Mom wrote to me before I was even born—"*...a sound that is your own yet carrying something of all the others ...*" I take a deep breath. "Yes."

Then I remember Mrs. Fensteen's purple face. "I have to phone Bridget and her mom, tell them I'm still going to play. Do you think they'll come?"

He chuckles. "You phone them. I'll bet they'll be pleased as punch."

"Mr. Franckowiak?"

"Yes?"

"Thanks."

"Anytime. Good luck tomorrow."

I hang up and touch the letter and look over at Dad. "I guess I'd better get the call to Bridget over with."

He nods. "How about you give them a call and then we'll have a little music. Not up in your room. Right here in the kitchen, where it belongs."

My heart beats hard as I dial the number on Mr. Dekker's student phone list, but Bridget answers the phone and she actually sounds kind of nice. "That happened to me once," she says.

"Really?"

"Except there are about eight hundred kids in my school. It's always the worst, playing for your friends. Hey, what about if we play facing each other? Then we can just think about the music and not worry about everyone out there."

"Great. Will your mom still drive you here? She seemed pretty mad."

"Oh, sure. She's always up for anything with applause and gushing teachers. But we can't take the Porsche. She was so upset after the practice that she backed into a fire hydrant, so we'll have to take the van."

After I hang up, I pick up the violin again. In the case is the photo of us at the Beaches. "Remember,

I got triple scoop and when I licked it, all that melting Rocky Road smudged up my glasses?"

He laughs too, the kind I remember from the night he made the maze. "She said, 'It's Hannah, shifting in from the Planet of Chocolate Marshmallows to—'"

"'To the Planet of the Waters Family,'" I finish. "She was always talking about you and me shifting in and out of different places."

"She liked to bury herself in other worlds—music and—"

"… music and music and the Corn Maze."

"Oh, and my spaghetti sauce, of course. She loved that."

"She did?" I laugh, and lift the violin. "I need to play now."

He strokes his beard and nods.

I tuck it under my chin. I play the Bach Double with all its shifts and twisting corners, and stand tall and sing my sound out the window to the stars. I make a note of the mistakes to go over slowly later, just as Mom taught me, and when I'm finished I look at Dad. He's smiling and crying at the same time.

"Oh, Dad," I say, going over to him and hugging him with all my might. I glance at my reflection in the window. Is it me? She seems different. A smaller nose? Taller? I quickly let go of Dad, rush to the window, and press my nose against the cold glass. Same big nose, same scrawny me. But I know she's out there somewhere. "Meet you tomorrow," I whisper to the blinking star.

Twelve

I CLUTCH THE QUILL she held so many times, dip it in the ink pot, and start to copy the final line of the first movement of the solo second violin part. I listen for the violin as if my head is the Hall of Mirrors in that hush before the performers come out on stage. *Listen.* I bury my head in my arms and scrunch up my eyes, just as I did in the pantry that day with the garlic hanging over my head. Silence ... just the tick of the clock, the house and everyone in it asleep ... then ... I hear it ... the sound of Papa's violin, but different, too, coming from a very long way away, as it did in the maze that day. I raise my head and copy the notes as I hear them, singing the first violin part as I go.

It's almost time for my solo at letter A. She goes first. Listen to her. *Listen.* It's like a game when she comes in a bar later, copies what I just said, except

higher. The whole school sits before us. And Dad ...
he's sitting in the front row with the hugest grin on
his face, the way he used to at my recitals. Listen to
the sound of Mom's violin. My violin.

Here's the bottom of the first page, where I
always get lost. I shift and climb up the scale and
throw the solo over to her like a ball ... fourth
finger vibrato! And listen to the first violin part
solo—is it singing I hear? Listen. There's Mr. F.
playing the piano part, steady as a metronome, and
Bridget's strong sound, so in tune ... but somewhere down in the middle of Bridget's tone is the
faintest trace of a voice, leaping over the octaves,
laughing, free. I close my eyes. It grows stronger, the
same voice I heard that time I was practising in my
room ... there's the girl, somewhere in a swirl of
dark ...! I dig my bow into the string for my solo at
C to answer back.

I make the fermata sign over the last note and place
the last sheet of music on Papa's table to dry. The
fermata looks like the eye of a bird. I smile a little
when I think of Herr Spiess playing this in a few
hours for the prince, sneezing on the bird and
sending it cawing and flapping angrily away. The

crows have begun to wake up—they're scrapping like crazy in the cherry tree outside Papa's studio window. I go straight to Papa's violin case and open it, touch the scroll ever so lightly, and then sing my way down the stairs to the mirror on the landing. It's very well dusted, like a clear lake with the light of a new summer day falling on it.

"Hello," I sing, fitting the words into the music. "Is that you playing Papa's concerto on Papa's violin?"

She nods and smiles.

I look straight into her eyes, which are clear and blue. Morning sun splashes over the mirror. I squint and think for a moment it might really be her—bigger nose … smaller bones? We have the same ache, though. I reach out my hand as if I could hold hers, listen for her sound, singing with all my might …

Here is the scary section near the end—all those notes in second position. It's like a long hallway with sharp turns and rooms and corners. What if I get lost, when I've come so far? Ouch. There was a note out of tune, and now I've missed the starting place of the D-string scale section. Jump back in!

Jump! It's her singing that helps me come back in at the right place. I give an energetic staccato thank-you and keep going, leaping over the last notes as if they're barbed-wire fences. I head into the final stretch. Home free. This last part is easy. If I can just hold on. I glance over at Dad in the front row as I shift down for the final bar. He's still grinning like a Ches-something-cat. I play the last D with the fermata over it, and listen to her voice on the same note.

⌣

I sing the last D, listening to the same note on her violin. After all that looping around each other and criss-crossing and back and forth, we finally sound together as one voice. And then ... the sun goes plain again, and there in the mirror is just me. Big bones, tall, Clumsy Catharina ... but look again— not really clumsy, that's just a name those rascal boys have invented, and what's so bad about being big and tall?

⌣

The applause bursts through the gym, and everyone jumps up and claps until we all have to bow a bunch of times. There's Mr. Dekker in the back row and Marie and Mrs. Franckowiak and Peppermint Woman. And Melissa and Brianne and Tracy are smiling, not whispering among themselves but looking straight up to the stage and clapping and smiling. And Dad in the front pushes up his glasses, still grinning.

"All I can say is … wow," says Mr. Griggs, his voice over the microphone breaking the applause. He motions for everyone to be quiet. "Thank you to our very own and very talented Hannah Waters—"

Everyone starts cheering and clapping again, and he has to break in. "Our very own and very talented Mr. Franckowiak." Loud cheers again. "And to our special guest, Bridget Fensteen." Everyone claps, and I notice Mrs. Fensteen along the wall, beaming and talking with one of the teachers. "We are indeed privileged to have heard such a fine performance in our school …

"We have another very special treat," he continues. "Yesterday I ran into Ms. Dumont, who is the great-great-granddaughter of Gabriel Dumont, which I'm sure our Grade 6 class will find of interest. She also plays the fiddle! She brought it today, and I'm going to ask her to come up to the microphone and play a tune for us, something from the Metis community."

She walks up to the mic and motions for me to join her.

"Come on, you can learn," I whisper to Bridget, and she follows me to the front.

"This is 'St. Anne's Reel,'" Marie says into the mic, and we're off, playing the tune for all of Clear Lake Elementary, Mr. Franckowiak pounding out the rhythm and chords on the piano, Bridget and me skipping notes and laughing as we go. At first, the audience just claps and stamps their feet. Then, Peppermint Woman—Peppermint Woman!—dances up to the front and pulls Mr. Griggs by the arm and starts to swing him around to the music. Ms. Lockport follows the cue and grabs Dad by the arm, and soon everyone's dancing—swinging and hopping and twirling around. It's complete chaos, but a good kind of chaos, Mr. Dekker swinging Melissa and Jeremy grabbing Mrs. Franckowiak by the arm, Ben hopping around with Mrs. Fensteen, who's taken off her high heels. The gym's echoing with laughter and screams, even Mr. Griggs's, and I'm right in the centre of it all.

After it's over, when the bell rings for recess, kids come up and give me high fives and say, "Way to go, Hannah," and ask me if I can teach them how to play.

"Hannah, that was *awesome*," says Melissa, snapping her gum, her face flushed from the dancing. "Can you come over sometime and play for our dance club?"

I glance at Bridget and Marie. "Sure. Maybe we can all come—you'd have your own private orchestra!"

"Excellent," she says. "See you later. We're over by the swings at recess practising our routine, so come over if you want." She exits with her gang.

People keep coming over—Mr. Dekker with quick congratulations before rushing off to a rehearsal, and Mrs. Franckowiak, who promises to take us out for a drive sometime, and Mr. Franckowiak, who promises to come over and play the piano as soon as it arrives at our house, and Mr. Griggs and all the teachers and Peppermint Woman, who's real name is Mrs. Betty Hodson Cunningham Walsh, who has to rush off to an IODE meeting, whatever that is, and Mrs. Fensteen, who has to rush off with Bridget, who has to get back to her school in the city.

Finally it's just me and Marie and Dad, walking out the big doors into the screaming, laughing playground, where lots of kids have unzipped their jackets because of the warm wind that began last night when I was running home and hasn't let up.

We're walking to Marie's car. She's going to give Dad a ride home, and he's taking my violin with him.

"We don't often get such a warm wind around here this time of year," says Marie. "Mostly it blows in Alberta." She lifts her face to the sky.

"I must say, I'm glad of a little warmth for a change." Dad peels off his gloves.

I hop over a muddy patch of snow, trying not to dirty my dress shoes, and notice a small, green shoot poking up through the dirt and snow by the sidewalk's edge. "Something green!" I shout and bend over it.

"It's a wild prairie crocus," says Marie. She and Dad come to kneel beside me. "The first thing to come up. Rare at the end of March, though, and especially in town. Usually they grow out in ditches, and not till April. Sign of an early spring. It's a beautiful colour—pale purplish blue."

"For you, Mom," I whisper, imagining that colour growing in the muddy snow, listening to the warm wind blow around us with the voice of the girl sending music through the air.

AUTHOR'S NOTE

HANNAH WATERS *and the Daughter of Johann Sebastian Bach* is a work of fiction, but Catharina Bach and her family were real people, and some of her story here is drawn from real events. For information about J.S. Bach, his family, his career, and life, I relied on many sources but am indebted to Christoph Wolff's book *Johann Sebastian Bach: The Learned Musician*. The death of Catharina's mother, Maria Barbara, did actually occur in Cöthen in July 1720, while J.S. Bach was away with Prince Leopold in Carlsbad. The historical accounts say that he left her healthy on his departure and returned to find her dead and already buried. There is a brief entry in the deaths register under July 7, 1720, that reads: "The wife of Mr. Johann Sebastian Bach, Capellmeister to His Highness the Prince, was buried."

One can only speculate who greeted J.S. Bach ẖ the terrible news, but for the purposes of this story, I have imagined it to be his daughter, Catharina Dorthea, then eleven years old and the eldest of four children, although "Tante Lena" (Friedelena), Maria Barbara's oldest sister, was living in the Bach household at the time and had lived with the family for almost a decade.

You can still visit the city of Cöthen (now spelled Köthen) in Germany and see the palace of Prince Leopold where J.S. Bach worked as director of music from 1717 to 1723. The maze and formal gardens are no longer there, however, but they did exist, as can be seen in the 1650 engraving by Mattheaus Merian of the princely palace and gardens. Although it is unclear for certain where the Bach family lived, it is thought that they lived very near the palace, some think on the Stiftstrasse ("Stift Street") number 11. You can still visit the St. Agnus Lutheran Church next door, where the Bach family attended.

Several of the musicians mentioned also really existed as part of the court orchestra—the violinist Joseph Spiess, the oboist and fencing teacher Johann Rose, the copyist Johann Colm, "two Monjou daughters," who were singers, and even the dancing master Johann David Kelterbrunnen. The prince's birthdays were great events celebrated at court, and J.S. Bach did compose cantatas expressly for these, including a duet from one cantata, "Heut ist gewiss ein guter Tag" ("Today Is a Good Day").

Catharina's father did compose the *Little Clavier Book* for Catharina's younger brother Wilhelm in Cöthen in 1720. This was meant to teach him not only keyboard technique but also to introduce him to the principles of musical composition. The original manuscript of the Concerto for Two Violins in D Minor by J.S. Bach is preserved in the library of the Jagielloński University in Kraków, Poland; copies can be found in music libraries, and many performers have made recordings of it. This piece was actually composed later than 1720, although the famous Brandenburg Concertos were composed during Bach's Cöthen period. Bach's second wife, Anna Magdalena, was a professional singer and also copied much music for her husband. While Maria Barbara left fewer traces, Wolff in his book mentions that she, too, came from a musical family and most likely would have also helped her husband with secretarial duties.

I am indebted to the wonderful Bach Memorial at Köthen Castle, where I was able to study up close many objects and instruments from Bach's time, including the "viola d'amore" of 1720 made by

Georg Aman, lute and violin maker from Augsburg. Bach was apparently familiar with this instrument, although my story of a violin by this maker falling into the hands of a contemporary violinist is fictional. The museum has published a guide through the Bach exhibition by Günther Hoppe, which also proved invaluable in my research.

———

The method used by Hannah's mom and Mr. Dekker to teach the violin was inspired by the Suzuki Method, founded by Dr. Shinichi Suzuki (1898–1998) and used worldwide to teach music to young people. I'm grateful to both the Method and to the Suzuki Association of the Americas, Inc. The sign on Hannah's mother's studio door—"Practise only on the days that you eat!"—is a paraphrase of a statement of Dr. Suzuki's.

———

The Latin poem by Martial was found in *Latin Prose and Poetry,* edited by George Bonney and John Niddrie. Thanks to Father Jerome Weber at St. Peter's Abbey for translating it into English.

ACKNOWLEDGMENTS

AN EARLIER VERSION of the first chapter previously appeared as "The Bach Double" in *When I Was a Child: Stories for Grownups and Children* (Oberon, 2003), edited by Eric Henderson and Madeline Sonik.

I am grateful to the Saskatchewan Writers/Artists Colonies (St. Peter's) and to Daphne Robinson for writing space and time. Thanks to the late Penny Robinson for inspiration.

For invaluable readings, critiques, and assistance, deepest thanks go to Rhea Tregebov, Jean-Marie Kent, Stephanie Bolster, Sue Ann Alderson, Holly Duff, Alan Crane, Aria Leroux, Cindy Nickel, and Marian Rose. Thanks also to Inge Streuber at the Bach-Gedenkstätte & Historisches Museum of Köthen, Arthur Janzen, Christopher Patton, Father Jerome Weber, Blanche Nickel, Marc Destrubé, and Ian Hampton for generous informational assistance. Thanks to my agent, Leona Trainer, to my editor,

Barbara Berson, and to the people at Penguin Canada for believing in the manuscript and turning it into a book. Special thanks also to Barbara for incisive critical feedback.

To all my family and especially to Bevan and Nicholas, thanks for love, patience, and support.